MURDER DRAMA WITH YOUR LLAMA

KATHY LOVE

ERIN MCCARTHY

ONE

I HAD AUDITIONED for a lot of roles in Los Angeles trying to get my big break. Young Blonde on Spring Break. Dead Body in Alley. Sexy Rich Girl. Nerdy College Student. I hadn't gotten any of those roles. (In my defense, I was pretty sure I only lost that first role because I was a redhead.)

But now, I found myself cast as Small-Town Maine Pub Owner.

Only this wasn't a role. It wasn't a movie or TV show. This was real life and I was speechless.

I stared at the clapboard building in front of me and blinked.

"You own a bar named Steamy's," my best friend from California, Oliver, said. "That better be a seafood restaurant reference and not anything else."

I didn't answer, too amazed to acknowledge his humor. It really did look and sound like a set, which was just crazy. Kind of cool. But crazy.

Out of the corner of my eye, I saw Oliver back up a few steps to view the whole building. It was a lot to take in. The pub appeared to be the first floor of the huge Victorian. Above that, there were two more levels, jutting up into the clear blue sky in a mass of dormers and scrollwork and even a turret.

Holy cow, I was also cast as the Owner of a Turret.

"You don't think this place is haunted, do you?"

This time, I turned to my friend and smacked his arm. "No! Don't say that. It does look like a great hangout for spirits, but I have to sleep here. I can't think about ghosts or I'll freak out."

Oliver gave me a look somewhere between sheepish and "whatever, girl," which frankly was as contrite as he ever was. Then he stared at the building again. "Soph, you inherited a freaking mansion."

I did. Suddenly, I felt more than just awe and wonderment. I felt a little nervous. What did I know about owning a pub? Or owning a house for that matter? A huge house, no less.

I swallowed a couple times, trying to calm the churning in my stomach. I could totally do this. I wanted to do this. I was tired of L.A. The superficialness, the crowds and the competitiveness. I wanted the clean sea air of a coastal town in Maine. I wanted to be a part of a community. I wanted trees and grass and the peaceful lifestyle that came with small-town living.

But just as much as all that, I wanted to get to know the grandmother whom I barely remembered. She had left me this amazing place and I wanted to do her proud. But I also wanted a glimpse into her life and who she was—or rather, who she'd been.

I could do this. It was just another role, right? Take on the pub, wear some Wellies, polish the brass knobs, eat some lobster, or whatever it was Mainers did.

My father always said my biggest asset was my unbridled enthusiasm. So time to be unbridled.

"Sophie? Sophie LaFleur?"

I looked around and spotted an old man standing on the covered porch near a door at the far side of the building. He was slightly stooped with a balding head and clad in a gray button-down shirt and gray dress pants. I blinked, hoping I wasn't seeing a ghost. Who knew my name. Then the gray man waved and smiled.

"You must be Sophie LaFleur," he called.

I nodded, finding my wits enough to wave back and head up

the walkway toward the porch. Oliver followed, so clearly he didn't think the man was a ghost. Oliver might act all cool and unflappable, but when it came to anything creepy, that was all an act. The guy had suffered nightmares after appearing in a local commercial for a Halloween superstore as a child.

The gray-clad man met us at the top of the steps, offering his hand as we reached him. I accepted, his hand feeling fragile and boney in mine. But his eyes twinkled, full of life, and I noticed he wore a jaunty red bow tie, which made him look quite dapper.

"I'd know you were Sunny LaFleur's granddaughter anywhere," he said. "You are the spitting image of her when she was your age."

His comment pleased me, even though I'd heard that before. From my mother. And my aunt. Although they both said it like it was a character flaw rather than a compliment, so seeing this elderly man say it with a wide smile, which exposed startlingly white teeth, was much nicer.

"So you knew my grandmother for a long time?" I asked.

He nodded, his grin growing wider. "I've known Sunny since grade school, so I guess you can imagine how long that must be."

My insides warmed. Already, I was meeting someone who could probably tell me a hundred stories about my mysterious grandmother. A person I only knew as a voice on the other end of a phone line, who I talked to occasionally in my younger years and who sent me Christmas presents that usually didn't meet my mother's approval.

In my childhood, I'd begged to go visit my grandmother but my mother had refused. Then as an adult, at first I'd been too broke to travel, then too busy filming almost three seasons of a television show, Murder, She Texted. I felt guilty I'd never made it a priority to head east and meet Grammy, as she'd insisted I call her.

"I'm Cliff Robichaud," the old man said suddenly as if it just dawned on him that he hadn't introduced himself. His attention moved to Oliver.

Oliver looked particularly punk rock today in his gray and

black buffalo plaid pants, tight Clash T-shirt, and burgundy combat boots. I'm certain my friend's bleached locks streaked with teal blue and his widely gauged earrings weren't something Cliff saw frequently here in quaint Friendship Harbor. But the elderly man simply smiled and held out his knobby hand.

Oliver accepted, and I sensed my friend relaxing a bit. He had wanted to make this trip with me, but I knew a rural small town wasn't really his scene.

"Silly Soph, there is no way I'm letting you trek into the wilds of Maine without me," Oliver had insisted. "Who's going to fight off all the bears and crazed lumberjacks?"

Truthfully, I knew it wasn't going to be him. He was a city boy, born and raised. A bear would send him running back to Rodeo Drive. And a crazed lumberjack? He'd either swoon or ask for his number. But I appreciated his concern and I was glad he was there.

I was no more a woodsman than Oliver. I had been raised in the Valley by upper middle class parents and I was as we spoke, wearing a California girl's uniform—skinny jeans, flip flops, and a T-shirt that said "Good Vibes." Everyone needs good vibes.

Oliver shook Cliff's hand. "Nice to meet you. I'm Oliver Maddox."

Cliff's eyes brightened even more. "Oliver Maddox? *The* Oliver Maddox, who starred in 'The High Jinx of Hayley and Jake?'

Oliver blinked, surprised and impressed. "Yes, that was me."

Now, it was Cliff's turn to look impressed. "I think I've seen every episode. My granddaughters loved that show. Never missed it. And I have to admit, even for an old guy like me, it was pretty darned entertaining."

"Thank you." Oliver was pleased, but I knew talk of the hit show from his youth was always bittersweet. Oliver claimed he'd already fallen into the "where are they now" category at the ripe old age of twenty-seven.

"I'm sure you are anxious to see the house," Cliff said, waving for us to follow. He headed back down the porch, his gait surprisingly fast for his age and his hunched frame. Spry was the word that came to mind. Probably the first time I'd ever used it.

He opened the door where I'd first spotted him and led us into a foyer, which had a wooden bench and coat hooks lining one wall. Coats for all types of weather hung on the antique metal hangers as well as several colorful scarves and a floppy straw hat. A pair of gardening boots with mud crusted on the soles sat beside the bench.

Cliff caught me studying them. "All of your grandmother's items are still in the house. I didn't pack anything up, because I wasn't sure what you might want to keep."

My grandmother's will had said that I inherited the pub, her house and all its contents, but the reality of those words hadn't really hit me until I looked at those muddy boots. Grandma had left me everything.

My gaze returned to those boots. Her boots. A wave of melancholy swelled in my chest, joining the other emotions of disbelief, uncertainty, and even excitement that I was finally here. Oliver touched my arm as if he was reading my jumbled feelings. He was good at reading me, although I'm sure all those sentiments showed on my face.

"So this door"—Cliff pointed toward a doorway just past a staircase with white ornate balusters and a dark wood handrail and newel post—"leads into the storage area and office of the pub and of course, then into the pub itself. But I'm going to let Dean show you around in there."

"Dean?" I asked. The name sounded vaguely familiar, but with all the other revelations of the last few weeks, I couldn't recall why or from where.

"Dean Jordan, he's the pub manager."

That's right. In the reading of the will, my grandmother had included that this Dean Jordan would continue on as the manager, which was fine with me. I had no idea how to manage a pub, so I was more than happy for the help. Besides, once Oliver returned to L.A. I would need a friend or two.

"The ladies seem to like Dean. Which is rough for an old guy like me. He's stealing all the good ones, leaving me the leftovers."

Wow. That was either a poor joke or Cliff was something of a jerk.

"Let me take you up to Sunny's home." Cliff climbed the straight, steep stairs, again moving like a man half his age. I followed, hand on the bannister and a little breathless once I reached the top. I needed to thoroughly take advantage of the fresh air and nature walks while I was here. Since deciding to give up acting after my show was canceled, I'd also given up my five-day-a-week workout regimen. It showed.

At the top of the stairs, there was another small foyer area. More coats and shoes lined this space as well. Cliff opened a white paneled door that had been painted dozens of times in the hundred years since this house must have been built. I could see other colors in the places where the current coat of white had chipped away. I stepped through the doorway and into a huge, country kitchen. The walls glowed a warm, sunny yellow and the floors were worn plankboard oak. Another sign of all the years this house had stood. The cabinets were painted a creamy white, but I could tell they were probably original too. I touched the glass knobs and admired the aged bronze hinges. Sunlight from several windows flooded the room, making the space warm and inviting.

The marbled gray granite counter appeared newer and gleamed in the sunshine. My fingers moved from the antique knobs to a nested set of mixing bowls perched beside a well-used mortar and pestle set. Suddenly, I could visualize my grandmother baking in this wonderful room. The smell of cookies and cakes wafting through the air.

"Sunny loved this kitchen," Cliff said from behind me. "She was a fabulous cook. She baked all the time."

I smiled over my shoulder at him. I knew it.

"She loved to make her edibles. She could outbake Martha Stewart when it came to her pot brownies. Delicious and potent."

He winked. "You two would have gotten along." He pointed to the slogan on my T-shirt.

My eyes widened, and a sharp laugh escaped Oliver, which he quickly tried to suppress.

"All purely for medicinal purposes, of course," Cliff added with a grin, his eyes sparkling.

I nodded, feeling like he might just be displaying "dad" humor. "Of course," I managed.

"Let's continue the tour." Cliff waved his arm out again. "I'm pretty good at this. Put me in a skirt and I could be one of Barker's Babes from the Price is Right."

Not dad humor, then. Grandpa humor.

As I followed, Oliver fell into step beside me, leaning over to whisper, "I think I'd have really liked your grandma. Chocolate paired with getting high is a win-win combo."

While consuming marijuana wasn't exactly scandalous in California anymore, it was still illegal in Maine. I shook my head. "I think he was joking."

Oliver raised a skeptical eyebrow, then linked his arm through mine as we followed Cliff. By the time we finished the tour, I knew Cliff hadn't been joking. I also knew why my mother wouldn't send me on an unsupervised visit to her. My grandmother had been one eclectic, and by her decorating sense alone, one eccentric woman. Her house was beautiful and wonderfully decorated, but gone were the images of a sweet, portly old granny. Now, I knew my grandmother had been an old hippie with a love for all things odd and mystical.

The exact opposite of my suit-wearing 100 Million Dollar Club real estate agent mother.

Oliver pointed to a large, vintage poster of The Grateful Dead over an antique, clawfoot tub in the master bathroom, then mimicked taking a hit off a blunt. I rolled my eyes but laughed.

My grandmother's bedroom was probably the most extravagant room in the house, decorated in gold and burgundy. An ornate four-poster bed draped in velvet took up the center of the room, which Cliff had referred to as the "magic maker," a descriptor I could have done without. On her nightstand, she had a stained glass lamp, a crystal ball, and a book still opened to the last page she'd probably read. Tom Wolfe's The Electric Kool-Aid Acid Test. I thumbed through it. The pages were dog-eared, and the cover faded. I had a feeling she'd read it many times. Definitely a hippie. Carefully, I set the well-loved novel back down, not wanting to lose her place. Of course, she wasn't going to be reading it, but somehow it felt right to leave it as it was.

A set of French doors that led out to a covered balcony saved the richly colored room from being too dark. I strolled over to them and peered out. The backyard looked like an English garden with riots of tangled wildflowers of every color haphazardly lining stone paths. In one corner, a small picket fence surrounded what looked like a vegetable garden. A picture of my grandmother in her muddy boots, tending her medical marijuana flashed in my mind. I grinned at the image.

Well, Grammy, you are turning out to be a whole lot more than I'd imagined.

Beyond the gardens sat two other, smaller buildings. I turned to locate Cliff, about to ask him if they were a part of my grandmother's property, when he spoke first.

"Let me show you around outside. I have quite a surprise for you."

"There's more?" At that point, if Grammy had a moat, I wouldn't have been shocked.

Only a week ago, I lived in a one-bedroom apartment with a bathroom where I couldn't close the door if I was sitting on the toilet and a kitchen where I couldn't open the dishwasher and refrigerator at the same time to this—a four-bedroom, two-and-a-half-bath Victorian mansion with porches and balconies and a glorious garden. What more could there be? This was amazing enough.

It made my impulsive decision to move to Maine seem less insane.

It felt *exciting*.

The sun shone down, full in the sky now as we stepped into the yard. It wasn't quite as warm as Southern California, but I breathed in deeply, enjoying the slight crispness to the air. Bees buzzed, birds chirped, only the sound of the occasional passing car interrupted their peaceful hum. No traffic, no honking, no endless drone of people talking far too loud on their cell phones. Just the rustling of the breeze in the trees.

Then the strangest sound I'd ever heard pierced the calm. A sound somewhere between a loud, long squawk and a small child noisily gargling. I shot a look toward Oliver. He'd frozen, mid-step, his eyes wide, his expression more than a little frightened.

"What was that?" he asked.

I gazed around, half expecting a wild animal or worse a cryptid of unknown origins to come charging out of Grandma's garden, hopped up on weed and paranoia.

Cliff paused to look back at us as we reluctantly followed him down the trail. "Oh, that's Jack Kerouac. I knew you'd be surprised."

"There is a dead writer's ghost living in your garden?" Oliver asked me. "I was thinking you might need to hire a gardener but now I think you need an exorcist."

There was no way that sound came from a ghost. But I was totally mystified and was about to ask for clarification when Cliff walked around the side of the building that was somewhere between shed and barn and pushed open a large door. Sunlight shone in through a window at the peak of the roof. Dust motes and a sweet, earthy smell drifted through the air.

At first, I only saw bales of hay and large bags of some sort of animal feed piled against the rough-hewn plank walls. Then I noticed a movement from within a gated stall across the room. And another noise, this time a low hum like a bass note on an oboe.

"It's okay, Jack," Cliff called toward the stall.

I saw more movement, then a white, wooly head with pointed ears and a long snout appeared over the stall door. The creature blinked with sleepy eyes, although it could have been its incredibly long lashes that gave the animal such a drowsy appearance. It rumbled again and stuck out the tip of its tongue.

"No need to be rude, Mr. Kerouac," Cliff admonished. "These are your new friends."

The animal replicated the sound a third time, only louder.

I jumped back instinctively while Oliver shifted behind me like I would protect him.

"Holy petting zoo, it's an alpaca," Oliver said, putting his hands on my waist.

"A llama," Cliff corrected. "You can tell the difference by their ears. Llamas have banana-shaped ears. They're also bigger than alpacas. This guy is three hundred pounds."

"And his name is Jack Kerouac?" I asked, curious, even as I was trying not to panic as the llama came up to the fencing and nudged Cliff like he wanted to be petted. "What is he doing here?"

Cliff grinned and scuffed the mop of wooly fur on the top of the animal's head. "Indeed. This is Mr. Jack Kerouac. Only the finest llama in all of Friendship Harbor. Well, to be fair, he's the only llama in Friendship Harbor. Still, he's one handsome fellow. He was your grandmother's pride and joy and Sunny's constant companion." Cliff rubbed the llama's head and gave me a look. "Llamas are social creatures. You'd better make nice with him. He's been lonely since Sunny passed and before that he lost Janis Joplin, so he's had a rough go."

Out of nothing more than instinct and rote obedience, I reached out and ran my hand over the llama's head. He was surprisingly soft. "I take it Janis was another llama?"

"You are correct. If I were you, I'd think about getting another pal for this guy. They're less likely to spit at you if they have a buddy."

Wait a minute. "I can't keep this llama! I don't know anything about taking care of it. Him. Jack. Kerouac."

"Sunny would roll over in her grave if you got rid of this guy." Cliff eyed me like I was a horrible human being. "Hay's here in the shed. Use the internet for the rest. That's what all you millennials do anyway. Can't seem to think without the internet telling you how to."

I didn't even have time to resent that because I was busy trying to imagine my life with a llama. I'd never had so much as a dog. My mother thought pets were dirty and needy. She hated going to friends' houses where her clothes would accumulate pet fur and dogs and cats might jump up on her. She forever lamented the insanity of taking living creatures into your home. I liked animals, unlike her. I'd longed for a dog or a cat or even a fish as a kid but the answer had always been no. As an adult, auditioning constantly and living in a tiny apartment, I had resisted the urge to indulge myself and get a pet.

One of my first thoughts in making this move to Maine was maybe I could dip my toe in pet ownership and get a cat.

Never, in a million years, would I have expected my first pet to be a llama. My brain was bouncing all over the place. "Did you say *spitting?*"

TWO

NOW, there was no doubt Sunny LaFleur was hitting the wacky tobaccy. A llama? My grandmother left me a llama? That might spit at me?

Said llama stuck out the tip of his tongue again as if to say he was no more impressed with me than I was with him.

Cliff flipped the latch on the stall door.

"You aren't letting him out, are you?" Oliver said, his eyes huge.

Ha! Not as amused now, are you, my friend? Of course, I knew my eyes were bugging out of my head too. I'd never been so much as within ten feet of a horse.

"Of course I'm letting him out. Big guy needs his exercise."

Jack made another of his hums, although this one was higher, more like a little purr of anticipation, and when the gate opened, he almost seemed to prance out as if to say, "that's right, uh-huh, I'm free."

I stepped back a little, still nervous of an animal this large, but he didn't show any interest in me. Instead, he trotted directly toward Oliver.

"What is he doing?" my friend called out, stumbling backwards away from the approaching wooly, white giant.

"Don't be scared. He's just curious. He generally likes new people."

"Generally?" Oliver squeaked.

The llama stopped inches from my friend and craned his neck to sniff Oliver's hair.

Cliff laughed and approached the nosy llama and terrified Oliver, who'd gone totally still.

"Here, give him this." The older man dug into his pants pocket and pulled out a peppermint, the soft kind that I normally only saw around Christmastime.

He popped the red and white sweet out of its wrapper and held it out to Oliver. "These are his favorite."

The llama's ears perked up, and he made a snuffling noise.

"Just place it in the flat of your palm and hold it out for him. He doesn't bite. Generally."

"I'm not really feeling this generally thing," Oliver said, but he took the candy and did as Cliff instructed.

Jack slurped it up, his lips and jaw moving side to side as he happily savored the treat.

I moved close. Jack really was pretty cute, I had to admit. Carefully, I pet his side. His ears twitched, but he didn't move away from my touch. I took that as a good sign.

Oliver grinned too, until Jack snorted, spraying a fine mist of llama snot into his face. I choked, trying to contain my laughter. Oliver shot me an annoyed glance, then wiped his face with his arm.

"Now, that he does do on occasion," Cliff said, not hiding his amusement either.

"Thanks for the heads-up," Oliver said, wryly, but then to my surprise stroked the animal's nose. Jack hummed again, and I already recognized that particular noise was one of contentment. Jack nudged Oliver's hand, searching for more treats, then shifted to sniff Cliff's pocket.

"Sorry, big guy, no more candies today."

Jack snorted again, this time without snot, as if he fully understood what Cliff had said, and wasn't pleased. He sniffed Oliver one last time, then ambled out to the fenced paddock and started nibbling on a patch of dandelions.

Okay, I could see why my grandmother loved this guy. I was already falling hard for Mr. Kerouac.

"We can let Jack graze for a while, I'll get you your keys and a list of phone numbers and such that you might need," Cliff said as he headed to the gate, we'd come in.

I was locking the gate behind us, when Oliver nudged me.

"I have to get a picture of this. There is no way our friends in L.A. are going to believe you inherited a freaking llama." He already had his phone out. He snapped a picture of Jack chomping away on grass, but as soon as his camera clicked, Jack looked toward us as if he knew exactly what we were doing. To my utter shock, the animal lopped toward us.

"No way," Oliver said, "he is coming over for a selfie."

I was pretty sure it was a coincidence, but it did look that way. Jack stopped at the fence, blinking his thickly lashed, brown eyes.

Oliver turned his back to the llama and held up the phone. "Get in here."

Jack rumbled.

"No spitting," I warned the waiting llama.

He lowered his lashes as if insulted by my warning. I stroked his nose, already worried about hurting the animal's feelings.

I turned and leaned in a little so I could see myself on the screen of Oliver's cell. Jack appeared in the background directly between us, again, just like he knew exactly what he was doing.

"Go Jack," Oliver said. Clearly impressed he snapped a shot. Then another. He scanned the final product. "I tell you what, that llama's got some mad selfie skills."

"I'm sure he's better than I am," I said. I was the worst at taking selfies. My expressions always looked slightly maniacal.

Oliver studied the photos a little longer, then nodded. "He really is."

I swatted his arm playfully, then pretended to storm away after

Cliff. He waited in the flower garden, but I saw he was no longer alone. He chatted with a man who appeared to be around my age. But it wasn't really his age that made an impact. It was the fact that this guy was gorgeous. Like "actor, model, possibly Greek god rolled into one" gorgeous.

"Holy Mary Mother of God, who is that?" Oliver murmured from beside me. I shook my head, still staring.

Seriously, this guy was the best-looking man I'd ever seen. And I was from L.A., for Pete's sake. The land of beautiful people vying for entertainment careers and investing heavily in gym memberships and healthy eating. I hesitated, a rush of nervous butterflies in my stomach, keeping my feet immobile. This was ridiculous. Sure, he was gorgeous. But gorgeous guys were a dime a dozen in Hollywood.

Play it cool, I was an actress after all—well. I'd *been* an actress before people with zero vision had canceled my show.

"Look who I found," Cliff called to me, forcing me to pull my act together and make my feet move. "Sophie, this is your pub manager, Dean Jordan. Dean, this is Sophie, Sunny's granddaughter."

Holy crap, this was Dean Jordan? I had imagined the pub manager to be a guy in his mid-forties with a beer gut and a dirty bar apron. Not the centerfold for a Calvin Klein ad. Okay, okay, he wasn't standing there in his underwear, but it wasn't hard to imagine. His black T-shirt and faded jeans did very little to disguise his broad shoulders, narrow hips, and abundance of lean muscles.

And his face. Perfection. A strong, chiseled jaw that was at odds with the full, sensual shape of his lips, a straight nose, and eyes the color of bourbon in front of a blazing fire. My admiring thoughts stopped as soon as I focused on those eyes. No, fire wasn't the right analogy. They were more like bourbon poured over ice. Hard and downright cold.

What had I done to warrant that cool reception?

He jutted his hand toward me.

"Nice to meet you," he said, his voice deep and smooth. I could easily have compared the timbre of his voice to bourbon too, but I was a little bummed by his curt greeting. He definitely was not the least bit pleased to meet me, which made no sense.

I refused to be intimidated by his less than friendly reception. This was one of those times when my plethora of casting call rejections came in handy.

I smiled widely, and my eyes met his, unflinching. "Nice to meet you too."

I accepted his hand, his long fingers encircling mine, his palms rough with calluses. Within nanoseconds, the touch was over, but my cheeks felt hot and I felt confused.

His gaze held mine for a few moments, then skipped past me to Oliver.

He nodded and offered his hand again. "Dean."

Oliver shook his hand. "Oliver," he replied, mimicking Dean's disinterested tone.

Not that Dean seemed to notice. Instead, he turned his attention back to Cliff. "I hear you are about to become a snowbird on us."

He sounded perfectly congenial to the older man, which made it all the more clear there was something he did not like about us. Maybe it was an outsiders thing? We weren't locals, so we were not worth his time?

I glanced at Oliver, curious about his first impression of my pub manager. Oliver returned my sidelong glance and rolled his eyes. Sadly, I had to agree.

"Yes, I'm heading to Florida in two days to settle on a condo in Ft. Lauderdale," Cliff said. "But I'll be back in a week, then leaving again mid-October. I've had enough of the cold and snow."

He gave me a rueful look. "I probably shouldn't lament the harsh, Maine winters, since you just got here from sunny California. I don't want to scare you away."

I heard Dean snort. "If cold and snow are enough to scare her away, then she probably shouldn't have come here in the first place."

"Oh, I'm not scared of the cold. Or snow. Or ice."

Dean looked thoroughly unimpressed with my declaration, and before I thought better of it, I added, "I happen to go to Lake Tahoe skiing every year, actually."

He cocked an eyebrow. "Well, you'll have to let me know how your first Maine winter holds up to a ski vacation."

Okay, my defensive comment did sound stupid. And decidedly L.A. of me. But I refused to be shaken by him. I continued to meet his frosty eyes, and even offered him a smile, until Cliff loudly cleared his throat, putting an end to the awkward exchange.

"Well, kids, I have a meeting I cannot miss today, so we should finish up with the house, and then, Dean, you can show them around the pub," he said, his gaze shifting between Dean and me. I'm sure he could tell that was probably going to be a less than welcoming tour.

"I have a few things I need to get done before I open the pub. Come after six," Dean said.

I honestly didn't want my relationship with my manager to start off totally contentious. I did need his help and so I was going to put in place my Sophie LaFleur Kill Him With Kindness Policy. It worked with even the crankiest of directors.

"That's perfect, I can't wait!" I said and gave him a dazzling smile.

My gesture wasn't met with any improvement in his demeanor. Instead, he raised his eyebrows like he thought I was bonkers. He mumbled a farewell to Cliff and started down one of the garden paths. And straight into the other building that appeared to sit on my grandmother's property.

"I don't know what that was all about," Cliff said. "Dean is usually a little friendlier, especially with women."

A little? He could be a *lot* friendlier and still be about as charming as the common cold.

"He lives next door?" I said, not pleased with the idea of

gorgeous Mr. Grumpy being my neighbor. I was bound to see more than enough of him at the pub.

"Actually, he lives in your guesthouse," Cliff said and gave me a wicked smile.

"HE LIVES IN MY GUESTHOUSE," I moaned as soon as Oliver and I were back in my grandmother's house, alone.

My house, I corrected.

"He's a tool," Oliver said sympathetically as he collapsed onto my grandmother's blue, velvet sofa. "But at least, he's nice eye candy."

"I don't want eye candy. I want nice, friendly neighbors. I want a fun and happy working environment. I wanted to fit in and feel a part of the town." I paced the room, picking up a candle and sniffing it. Lemongrass. I set it down. "You know my vision board says 'community' this year. You know, with the picture of all the people in a circle holding hands with each other at a small-town festival. That's what I want!"

"Well, he's just one person. You do have other neighbors around you. And presumably some of the other people working at the pub are friendly. He can't be the only employee."

"One person in a small town might as well be half the town. Everyone knows everyone. What if he convinces everyone to dislike me?"

He rolled his eyes. "Girl, what is this? High school. He's not going to do that. Besides, Sullen Stud Muffin was probably just having a bad day. Maybe his chainsaw is busted. Or he hit a moose, and his truck is all stove up."

"Stove up?" I asked with a laugh. Then I added quickly, "I like that nickname, by the way."

Oliver nodded his thanks. "Yeah, stoved up. I saw it in a Stephen King movie so it has to be legit Maine lingo. It means badly damaged. I think."

"You watched a Stephen King movie?" My supernatural-phobic friend kept surprising me.

"I had to know what I might encounter here," he said quite practically.

Maybe I should have thought of that too. You never knew. Ghosts didn't seem out of the realm of possibility now. Things had been pretty unexpected so far. I cast a look around my grandmother's eclectic living room with its dark wood floors and jewel-colored furniture. I studied a sort of strange tapestry on the wall with scantily clad Renaissance people dancing in a circle in the woods. It wasn't exactly scary. Different maybe, but not creepy. At least in the daylight. Ask me again after the sun set.

"Or maybe he had a bad morning lobster fishing," Oliver suggested.

"You do realize you are grossly stereotyping Mainers, don't you?"

"You're right."

My stomach growled, and I wandered into the kitchen. I heard Oliver get up from the sofa and follow me.

"But to be fair, any of those things could have happened. Not just in Maine. Probably in New Hampshire too. Maybe Massachusetts."

I shook my head but couldn't hide my smile. I did love Oliver. I was glad he was there. I didn't think I could have faced the day alone. "Are you hungry, you elitist city slicker, you?"

"I'm starving actually. Do you think your grandmother froze any of those brownies?" he said, heading directly to the freezer, while I checked out the cupboards. Cliff hadn't been exaggerating when he told us, upon departing, the house had been stocked with groceries as well as cleaned to get ready for my arrival. I wondered by who. I knew for sure it hadn't been done by Dean Jordan. I chose a box of snack crackers. Easy seemed best right now.

"Any luck?" I asked as I opened the top and headed to one of the wooden stools at the counter.

"Just ice cream." His expectant expression faded.

I laughed. "Well, I like ice cream."

"That's because you are a goody-goody."

"I am not," I said as if it was the worst insult I'd ever gotten. Because Oliver was right. I could be a goody-goody. Although I preferred to think of it as sensible, with a hefty respect for rules.

At times I had the sneaking suspicion half the reason I'd never found stunning success as an actress was because I wasn't willing to be shady. No couch castings, no partying with influencers, no casual cocaine habit. Obviously there were actors who did none of those things and had hit it big but generally speaking, it was not a world filled with straight arrows. I still liked to believe that hard work was rewarded and kindness was a gift everyone could afford.

I was a goody-goody straight arrow in an industry that didn't give out lollipops for that.

So my sensible and optimistic self was now in Maine, and honestly, it didn't feel wrong. Different. But not wrong.

Oliver sighed and took out the ice cream, looking like a kid who'd just opened his last Christmas present only to discover it was a pair of socks. As he searched the cupboards for a bowl, I turned on my grandmother's TV to see what streaming services she had.

That would be none.

"Do you want to watch a movie on my tablet?" I asked. "I need some chill time before I have to deal with the pub manager."

"That sounds perfect."

We sat at the kitchen table and ate ice cream and watched a romantic comedy we'd both seen about a dozen times. You could never go wrong with a rom-com.

"What is Ashton Kutcher up to these days?" Oliver mused. "I haven't seen him since middle school when I was still pretending I could have a girlfriend and I dated Rumer Willis for three weeks."

I opened my mouth to reply when a shrill ring filled the kitchen. I jumped, pressing a hand to my chest.

"What is that?" I asked, my voice breathy and my heart pounding.

The sound pierced through the room again.

Oliver pointed to a bronze dome edge with filigree over the door that led to the staircase we'd used when we arrived. "I think it's just a doorbell. The ghosts have you jumpy."

Again, it rang.

That was exactly what it was. Maybe Dean had decided to come over and tell me I was allowed in my pub now. Although it seemed like he'd just come through the office doorway Cliff had showed us and would knock on the kitchen door.

"See," Oliver said with an encouraging smile, "I bet that's one of your other neighbors coming over to introduce themselves. Maybe they brought over a pie or casserole."

I smiled. Maybe.

I got up to investigate, now that my heart wasn't threatening to leap out of my chest.

Oliver fell into step behind me. Did I mention I was very glad he was there?

I reached the foyer and opened the door, but it wasn't a neighbor, unless my neighbor was a cop. It was a female police officer in full uniform, gun and all. She looked very young, her brown hair pulled up in a bun and her pretty face devoid of all makeup. Freckles spattered her small nose. Honestly, she looked more like a young teen, playing a police officer. She stopped worrying her lower lips as soon as she saw me.

"Sophie LaFleur?"

I nodded, wondering how she could already know my name. "Yes."

"My name is Officer Young."

Well, that was certainly accurate.

"I need you to come with me. There's been an accident."

I frowned. I barely knew a soul in town, so why were they coming to tell *me*?

"What do you mean? What kind of accident?"

Was my pub on fire? I didn't smell smoke.

My llama missing? Jack was back in his pen.

A car smashed into my fence? That seemed plausible. "Has there been a car accident out front?"

"No. It's a personal injury."

"What? Who is it?"

"Cliff Robichaud, ma'am."

I gaped at her. "Oh my gosh, I just met him today. Is he okay? I was just with him two hours ago and he was perfectly fine."

"He's not perfectly fine now."

My stomach knotted. "Surely, he must have family and friends you should be making aware of this. Not me."

She nodded. "He does have family, but I still need you to come with me."

This couldn't be good. So much for being a welcoming neighbor with baked goods. Did they think I was somehow involved in his accident? And what accident could he have had? He'd seemed hearty and hale when he'd been giving me and Oliver our grand tour.

I shot a look over my shoulder to Oliver. He shrugged, as confused as I was.

"We need you to come get your llama."

I blinked. "Jack Kerouac?"

"Yes, your llama is at the scene of the accident, and he's being rather uncooperative."

That made more sense, then, why she was here. But it wasn't as if I knew how to wrangle a llama I had just met. Oliver nodded his head as if to say we better go get him. Or at least try to. I didn't know the verbiage for getting a llama to listen.

"Okay," I said, still feeling highly confused, but I followed the officer. She led us down Main Street, making a left onto Water Street, aptly named as it ran parallel to the ocean. If I hadn't been so confused, and frankly nervous, I would have enjoyed the beautiful old houses that lined one side of the street overlooking the rocky coast and harbor on the other side. But right now, all I could focus on was what was wrong with Cliff and how Jack had gotten out of his pen.

"Is Cliff okay?" I repeated, huffing a little to keep up with the thin, petite officer. She was making me feel old. Or reminding me how much I hated working out.

"Sheriff Pelletier will give you the details when we get there."

Oliver shot me a concerned look, validating my worries that this was not a good situation.

We continued down Water Street until we reached a dirt path marked by a wooden sign reading Friendship Harbor Walk. The path wound through a green tunnel of pine trees and maples until they gave way to a clearing and a spectacular view of the harbor. Despite my anxiety, I couldn't help but appreciate the beauty of the ocean crashing against the rocky cliffs.

Then I spotted a man in uniform, presumably Sheriff Pelletier. He waited farther down the path with Jack Kerouac, who was tethered with a rope, jerking his head in an attempt to get away.

"This is not good," Oliver said lowly, voicing my exact sentiments.

I broke into a run. "What happened?" I cried as soon as I reached the new officer.

Still struggling, Jack made a noise I hadn't heard before, a low, deep rumble. "What happened? Where is Cliff?"

The officer struggled with the rope, trying not to lose grip as Jack whipped his head again.

"You must be Sophie. I'm Sheriff Pelletier." He didn't offer to shake my hand, since he was rather busy with my irritated llama. "Jack is being ornery right now. Unfortunately, he was involved with a fatality."

"A fatality?" I gaped at the man. "Cliff?"

"Yes. Cliff Robichaud was found dead and it appears Jack Kerouac killed him."

"*What*?" Cliff had just been alive, feeding Jack treats. They were buddies, pals. How the heck could Cliff be *dead*?

I scanned the area, for the first time noticing another officer several yards away, talking to a tall, thin woman in her mid-forties, her movements jerky and frantic as she gestured toward my llama.

Then I noticed several feet away from me a damp, brownish-red spot on the pathway. Nausea hit me. That was blood. Blood seeped into the dried dirt. Cliff's blood.

"Are you sure?" I asked, even as I stared at the stain. I looked back to the sheriff, hoping he would tell me this was some bizarre joke.

He nodded slowly, his lips surrounded by a beard and mustache pressed into a grim line. "Cliff suffered a blow to his head. It appears your llama most likely kicked him."

Beside me, Jack rumbled again. Oliver moved to pet his side. Jack calmed, no longer tugging at the rope.

I opened my mouth, wanting to say something. But what did a person say when you discover your newly acquired pet just killed someone? The someone who was only one of two people you'd met in your new town?

As it turned out, I didn't have time to say a thing.

"Is this her?" a shrill voice cried, and I turned to see the woman that other officer had been talking to storming toward me. "Are you the clueless woman who let her dangerous animal loose to cause chaos in our town?"

"Karen, I know you are very upset," said Sheriff Pelletier, stepping in front of me before the irate woman could reach me. "But this was just a horrible accident."

"Accident? My father is dead."

My heart sunk. Oh my God, this was Cliff's daughter.

"I know," the sheriff said, his voice calm and sympathetic. "And I know how hard this is for you."

"My father is dead. Yeah, you're right, it is pretty hard." She glared around the broad frame of the sheriff at me.

"I cannot tell you how sorry I am." My heart ached for her and for Cliff. I pictured the twinkle in Cliff's eyes. His plans to spend winters in his new condo in Ft. Lauderdale. And although I knew I shouldn't, I even grieved for all the things I could have asked him about my grandmother. But more than anything, I grieved for the loss of Cliff in his family's lives. "I only got to meet your father briefly, but he seemed like a wonderful man."

Karen narrowed her eyes. "You knew nothing about my father."

I opened my mouth to agree, and that I could only imagine what she was feeling, but the stony, angry look in her eyes made me stop. Was she mad because her father died in such a senseless way? Or was she mad about something else?

"Karen, do you want Officer Young to drive you to your mother's? She will need to know what has happened, and I think it would be better coming from you than her hearing it from someone else," Sheriff Pelletier said.

Karen shot daggers at me for a moment longer, then frowned up at him. "No, I'm fine. I can go there on my own."

"Then I think you should head over there. You know how news travels around here."

I closed my eyes. Oh God, in a matter of hours, everyone was going to know my llama had killed poor Cliff Robichaud. This was awful. On so many levels.

Slowly, I opened my eyes to find Karen glowering at me again. She hated me. There was no missing that.

"You stupid flake. Why don't you just go back to So Cal, where you obviously belong?"

"Karen," Sheriff Pelletier warned.

But Karen didn't heed his warning, instead she lunged toward me, poking a long, thin finger toward me. I stumbled back, shocked by her sudden dive. Behind me, Jack Kerouac rumbled deep and loud.

Sheriff Pelletier snagged the irate woman around the waist, keeping her from coming any closer, but his restraint didn't dampen her rage.

"You have no idea what you have done," she shouted and struggled against the sheriff's hold. Fortunately, he was a big, muscular man and her struggles were fruitless.

Again, Jack rumbled.

"It's okay," Oliver whispered to the agitated animal.

But Jack didn't quiet. In fact, he made another noise, this one a loud snuffle. I turned just in time to see a spray of sticky, slimy mucus fly over my head and hit Karen, right smack in the face.

I groaned and closed my eyes. Oh, Jack. Just when I thought this day couldn't get worse.

THREE

THE PLUS SIDE to Jack's ill-manners was being covered in llama spit was enough to get Karen to leave. Not before she hurled a few more insults in my direction, but I couldn't bring myself to be offended. My llama had killed her father. I couldn't exactly expect to be besties after something like that.

"Are you okay?" Sheriff Pelletier asked once she'd stormed down the path in the opposite direction of the way that Oliver, Officer Young, and I had arrived there.

I sighed. "As okay as you can be when you discovered the llama you inherited is a murderer." I tried to smile but failed. "Honestly, I feel awful."

He smiled sympathetically, and I noticed for the first time, he was a good-looking man. Not the breath-stealing, mind-scrambling way Dean Jordan was. But he was very handsome. Facial hair peppered with hints of gray. Kind brown eyes. A nice smile. And he scored extra points for being nice.

"It was a freak accident. It's not like Sunny's llama has gone on killing rampages before. And Jack knew Cliff. Cliff cared for him whenever your grandmother was away. I suspect the old guy fell or something, and the animal managed to kick him."

I nodded, not that his explanation made me feel any better.

None of this would have happened if Jack hadn't escaped his pen. Karen had been right about that.

"Here," he said, handing the rope he still held to Oliver. "He seems pretty relaxed with you."

Oliver took it and started down the path. "Come on, you vicious beast."

Jack looked anything but vicious as he ambled along after my friend, his wool bouncing around his body like a bad home perm. The sheriff and I fell in step behind them, although I noticed we both left a wide berth between ourselves and the llama's back end.

"So, you are from California?" Sheriff Pelletier said suddenly.

I glanced at him. "Yes. L.A."

"I guess right now isn't the time to ask you if you are enjoying Maine."

He caught me off guard, and a surprised laugh escaped my lips. "No, probably not."

He smiled, then fell silent. I appreciated his friendliness, but I was glad for the silence. I was too shaken to make small talk.

We reached Water Street, and I noticed two police cars parked along the curb near the entrance to the scenic walk. I hadn't noticed them before. Officer Young and the other cop, whose name I still hadn't gotten, waited by one of the vehicles.

Sheriff Pelletier stopped near the other one. "I'm sorry this has been such a rough start to your move here. I hope it hasn't ruined things for you. This really is a nice, quaint little town."

I managed a smile. "It can only get better, right?"

He nodded. "It will absolutely get better."

A more genuine smile curved my lips. Well, at least the sheriff didn't seem to hate me. That was a start, I supposed.

"I'll be in touch if I need anything," he said. "But this all seems pretty straightforward."

I was glad for that, at least.

Both Oliver and I thanked him and continued down that sidewalk toward Main Street, walking Jack like he was a dog. We passed a few people who eyed us oddly, but they didn't stare at the llama in fear. I chose to see that as a good sign. Maybe the news hadn't spread yet that Jack had gone homicidal upon my arrival.

I let out a pent-up breath as soon as we got back to my grand-mother's house. My house, I corrected. The paddock door was still open, evidence of Jack's escape. Oliver led him back to his stall, then as if he'd cared for llamas all his life, he grabbed a pitchfork and shoveled in some hay for the animal and checked his water.

"I need a drink," Oliver said, when Jack was all settled. "I'm sure your grandmother's got a stash of booze somewhere."

"If not, there's a whole pub," I said.

"Good point." He left the barn, but I lingered with Jack. I curled my fingers into his fur, scratching his long neck as he munched on his hay, totally unfazed by the events of the day.

"I know I locked the gate," I murmured to the animal, replaying everything in my mind. "You'll see I'm a very trustworthy pet owner. Once, I took home the classroom hamster in third grade. You know, just for Christmas break, but I did great with that little guy. And not once did he escape. Or kill anyone."

I grimaced, realizing I was justifying to a llama.

And maybe I hadn't locked the gate. I had been overwhelmed by the tour of the house. And by discovering I was now the owner of a llama. Maybe I hadn't locked it completely. I rested my head against the llama's neck. Guilt filled my chest. Had my stupid over-sight led to Cliff Robichaud's death? That was a lot to handle.

"If only you could tell me what happened," I whispered to Jack. He responded by gobbling up another mouthful of hay, his jaw and lips moving side to side as he chewed.

I stroked his neck one last time, then left his stall, making sure the gate was securely locked. I shook it to be completely certain. I did the same with the gate of his paddock, trying to remember exactly what I did when I left it earlier. I just wasn't sure.

When I got into the house, Oliver had found a bottle of Jameson and two highball glasses. The ice machine on the door of the fridge churned and thudded as he filled with glasses with ice, then he returned to the counter and poured a generous portion of whisky into each of them. He held one out to me. I didn't usually drink liquor without plenty of mixer, but today, I was willing to make an exception.

Oliver raised his glass. "To Cliff. We didn't know you well, but you seemed like a nice man and we are sorry you had to go."

"To Cliff." I raised my glass. One swallow and I choked and shuddered and set the glass down. Oliver drained his. I just couldn't wrap my head around the fact that a man I'd just been talking to three hours earlier was dead. It was horrible.

"I could have sworn I locked that fence," I said, needing to share my thoughts with someone other than a llama. But even as I said it, I felt like I sounded like a child making excuses. After all, I just wasn't sure.

Oliver studied me. "There was a lot going on. It would have been easy to miss it."

I took another sip of the whisky, even though I knew I didn't like it. I grimaced, then slumped against the counter. So much for fabulous new beginnings.

"I mean, I didn't think to lock it either," he added, seeing my misery. "I was too busy with my phone to even think about it. Millennials and their selfies, right? Cliff was right about us. How predictable and gross. We've let down our generation."

He was refilling his glass when I grabbed his arm. Whisky sloshed on the granite countertop. "Soph! Watch it."

"Give me your phone," I demanded. His comment had triggered the realization that we could verify the gate.

"What?"

"Your phone. Let me see it."

He started to reach for it, then paused. "This isn't going to be some 'technology is evil' campaign, where you destroy my phone as a symbol of how our world is losing touch with humanity, is it?"

I held my hand out, waiting. He dug in his back pocket, typed in his passcode, then handed it to me. "I'm still paying on that," he warned.

I ignored him and tapped his photo folder, then swiped through his most recent photos.

"There," I said, waving the phone in his face.

He leaned back, squinting. "What am I supposed to see?"

I tapped the selfie of us with Jack, then spread my fingers on the screen to enlarge the picture. I handed him the phone.

He looked at it, his eyes widened. "The gate was locked."

"It was locked," I said, grinning, feeling as if a huge weight had been lifted off my shoulders. I had locked it. But my glee vanished immediately. It was locked, so who...

"So who unlocked it?" Oliver asked, finishing my thought for me. We both peered at the blown-up photo.

I took another sip of my whisky, this time barely registering the sour, burning taste. "And why? What would be the point of letting out a llama?"

"Could it have been Cliff?"

"He left ahead of us," Oliver pointed out. "He was talking to your Sex on a Stick pub manager."

He was right. But that also brought up a disturbing concern. "The pub manager who just happens to live in the guesthouse on the property. Feet away from the shed. Could he have gone in to see Jack and left the gate open?"

"I guess it's possible. But he looks like a man who knows his way around animals. That seems careless."

"Well, Jack didn't open the gate himself with his hooves, so who did? I can't stand the idea that people think it was me. I want to start a life here, not be the town murderess."

"Is it really murder if you didn't mean to do it? And it was a llama?"

I eyed my friend. "Okay, fine, that's probably manslaughter, but I still don't want anyone thinking it was my fault." I have this problem where I wanted people to like me. My mother wasn't like that at all. She did what she wanted and couldn't care less what people thought of her. Frankly, she *assumed* everyone liked her, because why wouldn't they? I had gotten none of that. I still wondered why Nicole Snowden hadn't liked me in the seventh grade. I'd been *really* nice to her.

"So ask the pub guy if he went in to see Jack. You're supposed to be meeting him after six, remember?"

I hadn't remembered. It had completely fled my mind when my afternoon had been interrupted by Death by Llama. "He does not seem like a guy who would take a stranger from California accusing him of being careless very well."

Oliver waved his hand. "Who cares? It's your property and he lives on it. It's a completely reasonable conclusion that he might have been the one who left the gate open."

I took one last sip of whisky. "Then let's go downstairs and talk to Dean."

"Let's do it. Show him who's boss."

WHEN WE ENTERED THE PUB, it was hushed and dark. The deep stained wood gave it a traditional pub feeling but it also contributed to the somber mood. A woman was behind the bar, softly weeping in Dean's arms.

Yikes. Grateful I was wearing sandals that were quiet on the wood floor, I made my way to the bar and sat down, clearing my throat so they would notice me. There was only one table with customers, a family of four, and one older gentleman down at the end of the bar.

The woman pulled back from Dean. She was an attractive blonde with an hourglass figure I kind of envied. I was shaped like a teen boy, long and lanky. She hastily wiped at her tear-stained cheeks and sniffled. "Can I get you a drink?"

"I'm Sophie LaFleur," I said. "I inherited the pub from Sunny, my grandmother." Which sort of made me her boss. "This is my friend Oliver, who's staying with me this week before heading back to California."

"Oh, Lord, I'm so sorry," she said, swiping away her tears. "It's just that I just heard the news about Cliff. I can't believe it. What a horrible way to go. But it's nice to meet you. I'm Brandy Hardeson. I'm a waitress and bartender here at Steamy's."

"I totally understand," I said. "I'm shocked about Cliff's passing and I just met the poor man today."

Brandy nodded. "I'm going to go check on my table. But let me know if I can get either of you anything."

"I'll take a menu," Oliver said.

I eyed him and he gave me a "What?" look in return.

"All we've eaten today is ice cream and whisky," he pointed out. "I can't function on nothing but sugar and booze."

He did have a point.

Dean hadn't said a word through our exchange. He just leaned on the back of the bar and brooded. He seemed to be really talented at that.

"I know the circumstances aren't ideal," I said to him. "But we do need to talk about how the pub is running. I don't want to interfere but I feel I should be informed."

I was trying to strike the right tone of firm but friendly. I was probably failing miserably but I needed to start somewhere.

"What would you like to know?" Dean asked. He shifted off the bar and pulled two glasses out from under the bar. He filled them with ice and used the tap to squirt water onto the ice.

"I'd like to know who is on staff, hours of operation, the menu, and the financials. I tried to do a little research before I left California but you don't seem to have a website."

Dean plunked a napkin down in front of me and Oliver and shifted the water glasses onto them. "We don't need a website. Everyone in town knows about the pub."

I was starting to feel like he was being deliberately obtuse. "Hey, after you saw Cliff this afternoon, did you see Jack? Was he out of his pen?"

Dean raised his eyebrows. "No. I went straight into the house though. I wasn't really paying attention."

"I'm just trying to figure out how he could have gotten out," I said. "The gate was closed when Oliver and I left."

I wasn't sure I had any reason to believe Dean. For all I knew, he'd let Jack out just to mess with the new owner, not thinking Cliff would end up dead.

"We have a pic," Oliver said, pulling out his phone. He found the image and turned his phone so Dean could see. "Definitely closed." Brandy put a menu down in front of him. "Oh, thanks, gorgeous, you're the best."

Brandy smiled at Oliver, looking flattered.

Dean studied the photo. I wondered what he was thinking about our selfie. I really did have a terrible habit of making the weirdest faces in those things. In this one, I looked a little bit like I'd been hitting Grammy's edibles. I felt mildly embarrassed. Brooding or not, he was still hot.

"Maybe the wind blew the gate open."

I didn't think a latch like that could blow open but I just sipped my water while Oliver perused the menu. "What time did you leave your place?" I asked, trying to figure out the timeframe. If someone had wandered onto the property, would I have seen them? Doubtful. Oliver and I had been mostly in the kitchen.

"Twenty minutes after I saw you. I just showered and then headed out. I went to Brandy's since she needed a ride to work. I was at her place for about an hour, then we've been here since."

I had a feeling that he and Brandy hadn't been discussing ways to improve the pub's profits. Even though his expression was neutral, the comforting hug and "hanging out for an hour" pointed in the direction of them dating and a little pre-work afternoon delight. And I didn't mean going for ice cream.

So if he was busy hooking up with Brandy, did that mean I could believe him? It did seem unlikely that he would have had time to go hang out with Jack before his meet-up with the waitress. I made a mental note to find out where Brandy lived and how far of a drive it would be to the pub. Then I did a mental face-palm. What was I trying to prove? Was it just that I wasn't responsible for Cliff's death?

Or holy moly, was it possible someone had murdered sweet old Cliff?

I took a huge gulp of my water.

"Can I get some fried clams?" Oliver asked.

Dean nodded.

"I just feel so bad about Cliff," I said, trying to ferret out any information about him that I could. Was he someone another person would want to murder? "Was he well liked? He seemed like a charming guy."

"Men liked Cliff. He was easy to get along with and a hard worker. Women liked Cliff until they didn't."

"What do you mean?"

"He ran through women like toilet paper. They would fall hard for him, then he'd eventually move on, and then they hated him."

Interesting. Goes to show there was no age limit on players. But before I could move on to someone else being involved, I had to be sure Dean's alibi held up.

"So I don't want to be nosy, but are you and Brandy dating?"

Dean paused, wiping down the bartop. "That seems pretty nosy for someone who doesn't want to be nosy."

He'd called me out, but I pressed on.

"Well, I'm just curious. I mean hanging out at her house for an hour? That seems like a long time to be there. You know, if you were just picking her up for work."

Dean stared at me for a moment longer, then tossed the damp rag he still held in the sink. "I should let the cook know about that order of clams."

As soon as he disappeared through a swinging door into the kitchen, Oliver turned to me and hissed, "What are you doing?"

"I need to be sure Dean's alibi is solid. We can't look into other suspects until we rule him out."

"Other suspects? What other suspects? The police suspect your llama. All solved."

"But someone let Jack out. We know that." I gestured to his phone.

"Okay, so Dean says he wasn't even around at the time. That doesn't mean someone else didn't wander up and let out Jack."

"But why?"

Oliver frowned at me like I was crazy. "You can't think someone let out your llama to use him as a lethal weapon?"

"Maybe not as a weapon. Maybe as a decoy from what really happened. Remember on the fourth episode of season two of Murder, She Texted, the killer used the victim's extreme allergy to cats to disguise the reaction of the poison he used to murder her?"

Oliver gaped at me for a minute, then said calmly, "No. No, I don't remember that. You do know I only encouraged you to come down here to confront Surly McSteamy just to absolve you of any involvement when it came to the locals. I didn't expect you to decide there was somehow foul play." He made air quotes.

"Surly McSteamy." I nodded approvingly, undetermined by his tone. "That's a really good one. Nice play on the name of the pub too."

"Thanks."

"I just think there is something off about all this," I said. "And he did say that Cliff had a lot of women who hate him."

"Soph—"

"Did you decide on something to eat?" Brandy said from behind us, causing us both to jump.

"Oh, um, Dean took my order," Oliver said.

"So, how long have you and Dean been dating?" I asked as soon as Brandy came around the bar.

Brandy gave me a puzzled look. "We aren't dating."

I glanced at Oliver pointedly as if to say, "see, Dean's timeline doesn't make sense." Oliver rolled his eyes.

"We've been friends for years. He's a huge help with my son. Like today, he watched Ethan while I ran some errands before work. Ethan's dad is a total deadbeat, and Dean has always been there to help me out. But we've never dated."

A strange rush of relief coursed through me, which was, of

course, solely because I could trust Dean's story. It certainly had nothing to do with him still being potentially single.

"Wait," Brandy said, her brown eyes wide with concern. "You aren't going to prohibit coworkers dating, are you?"

"No," I said and she immediately looked relieved.

"Oh good, because I'm supposed to be going to a concert with Chad."

I nodded, happy for her, although I had no idea who Chad was.

"He's the new dishwasher," she added, probably seeing my confusion. "I have terrible taste in men, so who knows where it will go anyway." She shrugged and moved to fill a pint glass with beer, then headed down to the old guy at the end of the bar.

"Well, I doubt she's a suspect," Oliver said wryly. "She clearly isn't the tight-lipped type."

I nodded. It was good to know I could check one person off the list of suspects. Not that I exactly had a list. Yet.

Dean reappeared with a plate of clams in hand. He set them down in front of Oliver. "Can I get you anything else?"

"No," my friend said quickly, obviously trying to stop me from further questions.

Dean reached under the counter and set out two sets of utensils wrapped in paper napkins for us, then turned to leave, but he only took a couple steps before returning to us.

"Listen," he said, his expression still unreadable, "I get the feeling you think I messed around with the gate. But I'm telling you straight up I didn't. And I'm also telling you I'd be man enough to cop to it if I did. For the record, Sunny loved that llama and I'd never let him roam around town just to play some stupid game with you."

I met his gaze, and though his eyes were still cool, I could see truth in them. I could also see they weren't just a golden amber color. They were flecked with green. Like seriously gorgeous green. I nodded.

He nodded too, then left to go back into the kitchen. Behind me, I heard more people enter the bar.

Oliver let out a low whistle. "He's enough man alright."

I elbowed him, but smiled. "Okay, so I believe Dean didn't let the llama out. But someone did. And I'm going to find out who and why."

"Good luck with that," Oliver said, then popped a fried clam in his mouth. He made a face of approval, then nudged the plate toward me. I tried one, and moaned with appreciation.

"Wow, those are amazing," I said.

Oliver responded by pulling the plate back in front of himself and eating another one.

"Just so you know, I'm not going to need luck," I told him. "I'm going to figure this out with some good, logical detective work."

Oliver frowned and chewed.

"But not until I get some of those clams too." I waved to Brandy to place an order.

FOUR

"I REALLY DON'T SEE what we're doing back here," Oliver said, trailing reluctantly after me.

I strode down the dirt path through the canopy of trees. "I think we should take another look."

"A look at what?"

"The crime scene."

"Doesn't there have to be a crime for it to be called that?" he pointed out.

"I just think we should be sure. If Cliff's death was a crime, there are bound to be clues."

"If Cliff's death was a crime, the police would have had the scene roped off and they would be the ones looking for evidence."

Oliver did have a point, but something told me I need to be certain. What if something was missed?

As we reached the place where Cliff had died, the wind started to gust in from the ocean, the air chilly and damp. Clouds rolled over the gray, rough water.

"I feel like a heroine in a gothic novel," I said, pushing my windblown hair out of my eyes. "A stranger in the wilds of Maine with no one to trust. Well, you know, aside from you."

Oliver shot me an exasperated grimace. "I feel like this is

creepy. A man died here today. And it looks like it's going to storm."

"All the more reason to look for any evidence now." I started inspecting the dirt path.

"What evidence?" Oliver wasn't hiding his annoyance. But to my surprise, he started scanning the ground. He knew I wouldn't stop until I fully investigated the area. Silently, we searched the area around the now faded splotch of blood.

After a few moments, Oliver bent down and started to reach for something along the edge of the path, where it turned to grass.

"Wait!" I cried and he jumped. "Don't touch anything."

I pulled a set of plastic gloves and a Ziploc bag out of my back pocket. I held the items out to him.

Oliver stared at them, then gave me a puzzled, and slightly concerned, look. "Where did you get those?"

"I snagged them from the kitchen in the pub when Brandy brought me back to meet Jimmy the cook and Chad. You know the new dishwasher. Which by the way, Brandy wasn't lying, she clearly doesn't have the best taste in men. I mean he seemed nice enough, but she could definitely do better." I sighed, immediately feeling guilty. "I really shouldn't make such a snap judgment though, should I?"

Oliver continued to look at the gloves and baggie as if I was offering him a big, hairy spider. "You stole them from the kitchen."

I made a face as if he were crazy. "Of course, I didn't. I asked the cook if I could take them."

He still looked somewhat appalled. "I'm sure he didn't find that random. Soph, you are taking this all way too seriously."

"Of course I am. It is serious, and if we find something important, we can't risk contaminating it."

Oliver shook his head, but took the items. He tugged on the gloves, then picked up the object he'd discovered. He looked at it for a second, then held it up for me to see. "Thank God I didn't contaminate this old bottle cap."

"You know, sarcasm isn't always a good look on you. Put it in the bag. You never know, it might be something. What if the killer always drinks..." I read the top of the cap through the wrinkled plastic as he dropped it in the baggie. "Moxie. What the heck is that? See, that has to be unusual."

"I'm sure Moxie will be the smoking gun."

"Sarcasm," I pointed out as I moved off the path. The tall grass swayed and bent in the breeze, so I moved slowly, brushing aside the blades and weeds with my feet.

"Does a candy bar wrapper count as evidence?" Oliver asked, holding up the crumpled plastic foil between his fingers.

"Yes, bag it. It might have traces of saliva." I slipped back into my role as Jennifer Flescher easily.

He grimaced and shoved it into the bag.

I returned to toeing at the grass, but after several minutes of searching, I hadn't found so much as a wrapper. I couldn't get discouraged. This was a slow, systematic process, not a mystery designed to be wrapped up in a sixty-minute time slot. With renewed determination, I continued for several minutes, when Oliver made a gagging noise from behind me. I stopped and dashed to see what he'd found.

"I think it's a fingernail." He cringed and pointed to a spot in front of him.

I peered down at the small, oval thing in the gravel. "It does look like it. Pick it up."

He pursed his lips and rapidly shook his head. "Mmm-mm, I'm not touching that. There are limits to friendship and this is it."

I sighed and leaned down to snag the small object, not an easy task since my gloves were far too big for me and a good length of plastic flopped past my fingertips.

"Got it," I said after several attempts. I dropped it into the palm of my other hand and we both stared at it. It was definitely a nail. A press-on type colored a creamy pale pink. Bits of dirt stuck to the adhesive on the other side.

"Thank God it's fake. I could not handle a real nail." He shuddered dramatically.

I wasn't sure if I could either. But I didn't share that with him. I was supposed to be the fearless leader in this instance. Instead, I nodded approvingly and said, "Good eye."

Oliver didn't appear to appreciate the compliment as he went back to scanning the ground, his expression decidedly grim. I started to go back to the grass, when I stopped. I needed to take in the whole scene. Like the main character in Murder, She Texted, I had to visualize how the crime might have happened. I studied the dulled stain of blood. Which direction had Cliff been walking?

I assumed, since he'd left my house not long before he was struck, that he must have been heading the same way we had entered the park. And probably the person came up from behind him. I squinted at the ground, noticing many scuffs in the dirt. There were several in the area where we'd been with Jack and where the confrontation with Karen happened. But then I noticed longer marks just beyond the blood, two on either side of the stain. As if maybe Cliff had put out his hands when he'd fallen. If that was the case, then he had been heading the way I thought. Away from my house like I suspected. And if he was hit from behind, maybe there would be evidence also in that direction.

I headed that way past the bloody spot, looking closely for anything. And then I saw something at the edge of the path, closer to the side overlooking the cliffs. I rushed forward and picked up the object.

"Did you find something?" Oliver called from where he'd taken over inspecting the grass.

"Yes." My heart thumped with excitement. This had to be something. Something important.

He joined me, inspecting the object.

"What is it?"

I shook my head. "I have no idea."

It was a gray cone that reminded me of a miniature flower pot. There was a hole in the narrow end. The thicker end that looked like the top of the pot had shallow circles on the bottom, but was solid otherwise.

"Is it some kind of cork?" Oliver said, picking up to look at it closer.

"It could be. Maybe he was hit with a wine bottle."

Oliver looked dubious, then handed it back to me. Clearly he wasn't convinced that my discovery was anything important, but that didn't diminish my thrill. It was a clue. I was sure of it. Happily, I dropped it into the baggie with the other items. I went back to checking that same area closely, but after about ten minutes and no more discoveries, Oliver groaned loudly.

"Do you feel that? It's starting to rain," he called over the wind and crashing waves.

I focused my attention on the sky. It was getting grayer and darker. And chilly. I realized I had goose bumps, although I hadn't even noticed in my determination to find more clues. I pushed my whipping hair out of my face, feeling it was already damp from sprinkles.

"You're right. Maybe we should head back to the house." I stuffed the bag of evidence into the front pocket of my jeans.

"Hallelujah," he said, already heading down the path. I jogged to catch up with him.

By the time we reached my grandmother's house—my house— the rain was coming down in a steady drizzle. The lights in the pub glowed warmly and through the windows I could see there was a bigger crowd there than when we left. Bustling for a Thursday night. Good to know.

I started up the stairs, then stopped. "I should check on Jack before I go in."

"Have fun with that. I'm going inside to dry off and put on something warm." Oliver waved with no signs of guilt as he headed down the porch to the door.

I stuck out my tongue at his back as he disappeared inside, but couldn't really blame him. I'd rather be doing the same thing, but I was now a pet owner and I needed to be sure Jack was all set for the night. I walked back down the steps and across the narrow front lawn. The rain chose that moment to go from drizzle to full downpour. I ran as fast as my flip-flops would allow on the slick, wet grass. As I rounded the corner of the house and Jack's shed and pen came into view, barely visible in the waning light, I slowed. Then I blinked. And blinked again, but both times I saw the same thing.

A dark figure stood near the gate.

I must have made a noise, because the shadow shifted, then took off across the lawn, racing down the length of the fence into the line of trees that separated my property from the neighbor's.

"Hey!" I called and started to run after the featureless form, only to stop rather gracelessly at the pen gate, catching myself on the handle before I wiped out. Stupid flip-flops. But what was I doing anyway? It was sheer lunacy to chase after a creepy, lurking stranger by myself in the dark.

"Is everything okay?" a voice said from behind me, and I screamed and jumped. I spun around to see Dean, his handsome profile half illuminated from the lights from inside the house and the pub.

"Oh my God, you scared me," I said with a shaky laugh. "But I'm glad it's you." I never expected to say that.

"What happened? I heard you yell."

"I was on my way out to check on Jack, and there was a person standing here by the gate. He—or she—I couldn't really tell, ran that way." I pointed in the direction where the figure disappeared.

"Really?" Dean frowned. He cast a searching look into the darkness. But aside from the patter of rain on the roof of Jack's barn and the low hum of the music and conversation in the busy pub, there were no other sounds to be heard. And no movement.

"I scared him--or her--off," I said after a moment.

Dean nodded, although even in the dim light, I could see he was skeptical.

"There really was someone out here," I told him firmly. "I know you probably think I'm a flaky, L.A. actor-type like I'm sure most of the town does by now." I knew they did if Karen had anything to do with it. "And to be honest, I can be flaky at times, but most people can be, you know. And I am most definitely not being a flake right now. Someone was standing right here. And someone did let out Jack today. And frankly, I'm a little freaked out."

He stared at me for a few moments, and his silence only added to my already rattled nerves. But before I could tell him that he could just go back to the pub, that I was fine, he said, "I believe you."

It was my turn to stare. "You do?"

He nodded.

I was speechless. This was the first time I'd felt any connection with him. Finally, I just opted for, "Thank you."

"Let me go with you to check Jack. I'm sure it was nothing. Just someone messing around. Maybe even someone from the pub who wandered over here tipsy, but I'd feel better if you had someone with you."

"I would too," I admitted.

Dean opened the gate and stood back to let me enter first. I hurried to the shed, ready to be out of the rain. The shed was very quiet. No snuffles or hums or rumbles. And as I approached the stall, I realized Jack hadn't appeared at the stall door.

Great, my llama was loose again. In the rain. At night. God forbid he killed someone else. Not that I believed he did the first time.

But was Jack being set up a second time to be a scapegoat?

To my relief, when I rose on my tiptoes to get a better look in the stall, I found Jack lying in his hay, his legs splayed out like a fat bullfrog and his head and long neck stretched out in front of him. His heavily lashed eyes were closed.

"Oh my God, is he dead?" What if that was what the stranger had been doing here. Killing my llama.

"I'm pretty sure he's sleeping," Dean reassured me. Jack twitched an ear to confirm.

I had to be sure he was okay. I couldn't leave him if he was dying a slow death from poison. Or a wound I couldn't see. I unlocked the stall door, and Jack opened his eyes, blinking groggily. Then he lifted his head, although he didn't look any more thrilled with being woken up than I usually did.

"Sorry, buddy," I murmured to him as I stepped into his stall. "I just want to be sure you are alright."

He bobbed his head slightly, which I took to mean he was okay with my intrusion. I pet his head and rubbed his ears. He hummed. Carefully, I walked around his still splayed body.

"What exactly are you looking for?" Dean asked, a mildly amused look on his handsome face.

"I'm not sure," I admitted, shoving back my tangle of sopping wet hair. I was pretty sure I didn't look nearly as good soaked as Dean did. "Blood or something."

Upon saying that, a thought hit me. I leaned over and inspected the llama's feet. "Wow, did you know Jack doesn't have hooves? They're like two big toes with thick toenails."

"I never really noticed," Dean said, and I had the feeling he was trying not to laugh at me. But I didn't look to see. Instead I lifted Jack's foot, trying to see better.

"What exactly are you looking for now?"

"Blood," I repeated more assertively. I looked up from prodding Jack's back foot. "If he kicked Cliff hard enough to kill him, wouldn't there be blood on his feet?"

"I guess." He glanced toward the shed door as if he wanted nothing more than to get out of there. But he stayed put and met my gaze. "Sophie—"

A tingle of awareness danced over my skin. My name sounded really interesting said in his deep, smooth voice.

"Why do I get the feeling you don't think Cliff's death was an accident?"

"Because I don't," I said simply. I moved to study Jack's other foot, poking at the pads. Jack rumbled, and I hurried my examination, recognizing that particular noise as a warning the animal was annoyed. I didn't want to add spit to my drowned rat look.

"I'm sorry." I pet his wooly back. "I know it's very rude to be woken up and then poked and prodded." I scruffed his head, then left the stall, locking the door securely.

"No blood," I said, giving him a pointed look. "Don't you find that odd?"

"Not really. He could have walked it off. Or he could have kicked Cliff so swiftly, he didn't even get any blood on him."

"Maybe," I agreed, even though I really didn't.

Dean stared at me for a moment, then shook his head as if he had no idea what to make of me. "Let me walk you back to the house. I need to get back to the pub. We're pretty busy tonight."

"Is the pub usually this busy on Thursday nights?" I asked as we stepped outside. The rain had returned to a light drizzle and I could easily hear the beat of a classic rock song and the chatter of patrons.

"Yeah, usually."

"Fridays and Saturdays must really be hopping."

He nodded. "We're definitely the popular spot for locals."

Locals. That was good. I could get to know some of them and possibly get some more intel on how people really felt about old Cliff. "I'd like to start helping out tomorrow."

He didn't say anything for a moment, but when he did, I couldn't miss that the lukewarm friendliness had left his voice. "We're open for lunch tomorrow. Brandy has to take the afternoon off, so I guess I could use some help for that shift."

Despite the returned coolness of his tone, I shot him a wide smile. "Grea—"

Unfortunately, the combination of his personality shift and my attempt to continue to kill him with kindness didn't mix well with walking, wet grass, and my flip-flops. No sooner did I flash him a huge smile, my foot slipped. One leg slid out in front of me, and I was in imminent danger of doing the splits. A move I couldn't do. But before I fell on the wet lawn, my legs contorted in awkward angles, his strong arm caught me around the waist and I was pulled tightly against his side.

"Are you okay?"

I nodded, trying desperately not to notice how warm and muscular and amazing he felt against me. He even smelled wonderful, like Christmas morning, all pine and spices. I closed my eyes for a moment, breathing in deeply. Then I remembered he'd asked me a question, and my eyes popped open.

"Yes, I'm fine."

He looked down at me for a moment, his expression back to unreadable. Then he practically lifted me away from him. Neither of us spoke the rest of the way to the back porch of my grandmother's house.

My house, I corrected.

Once I was up the steps, I turned to thank him. "Oh, and what time should I be there tomorrow?"

"Noon is fine. Hopefully you won't have a repeat of tonight while carrying a tray full of food."

It took me a second to understand what he meant. Oh, my clumsiness. My cheeks burned, but I managed a cheeky grin. "No promises."

I fought the urge to palm-smack my forehead after he walked away with nothing more than a cock of his eyebrow and a look of general concern. He clearly thought I was an idiot.

I released a dismayed sigh and tried the door. It was locked, so I knocked and waited.

The door unlocked almost immediately, and Oliver stood there in a hoodie, sweatpants, and thick socks. If envy really turned a person green, I'd have looked like the Wicked Witch of the West. I glanced down at my soaked T-shirt and jeans. Specifically at the moment when Dorothy threw the bucket of water in her face. What a world. What a world.

"Were my eyes playing tricks on me, or did I just see you get chivalrously swept into the arms of your resident hunk?"

I rolled my eyes. At least the heat in my cheeks was warming me up a little. "You would have to see that."

"I was spying," he admitted happily. "How did you happen to run into him?"

"Let me get into something dry and I'll fill you in." I made sure the door was locked, then headed toward the stairs to the upper level.

"Your bags are in your grandmother's room," he called after me.

Oliver was probably going to continue to tease me mercilessly about my near wipeout and Dean's save, but at least he did bring in my luggage. I could hug him for that.

I hurried toward my grandmother's bedroom, which was at the end of the long hallway. The corridor was lit only by three sets of wall sconces. The kind with the bulbs shaped like fake candle flames.

A shiver snaked through me, and it definitely wasn't just the cold. Who had that dark figure been? And what were they doing? In my grandmother's mansion of a house, the person's presence was even more unsettling. Being in a gothic novel suddenly seemed much less appealing.

I groped around on the wall inside my grandmother's room, finding a light switch. A chandelier in the center of the ceiling turned on. Refracted light shimmered through the dangling crystals and over the walls. The effect didn't exactly calm my nerves.

I located my suitcase. Quickly, I lifted the heavy satchel onto a tufted, velvet bench at the end of the canopy bed, unzipped it and found a sweatshirt and a pair of fleece pajama bottoms. I glanced at the French doors that looked out to the garden. I didn't think anyone could see in with the balcony there. But what if someone was on the balcony? Not likely since it was on the third level and not accessible. Still, I took my dry clothes and headed to the bathroom.

Seconds later, I was bundled in heavenly warmth, and I sped back down to where Oliver sat on the sofa in the living room. He didn't look the least bit nervous. Which tipped me off that he couldn't have seen the shadowy figure.

I collapsed into a chair and told him the whole story.

"Did Dean see the person?" Oliver asked. As I expected, he no longer looked quite as relaxed. He got up and pulled closed the drapes on either side of the French doors.

"No. But he did say he believed me. He thought it was nothing though. Just someone messing around."

Oliver considered that.

"He's probably right." He didn't sound any more convinced than I was. He sat back on the sofa. "I say we watch a movie, and try to relax." He reached for his tablet on the coffee table and I moved over to sit beside him.

"Nothing scary and no mysteries," I said and he nodded in agreement.

"Pitch Perfect, it is."

I'M NOT sure when I fell asleep, but I woke up after making it through Pitch Perfect and half of Pitch Perfect 2. Oliver slept beside me, his feet up on an ottoman he'd pulled over from one of the oversized, velvet chairs. I straightened upright from where I'd been sleeping on his shoulder. I peered around, disoriented and bleary.

Carefully, I eased off the sofa to go into the kitchen and get a drink. I found bottled water in the fridge, opened it and took a long sip. I checked out the contents of the fridge and decided I wasn't hungry. Taking another drink of the water, I wandered back to the living room. Somewhere in the house, I heard a clock ticking, but otherwise, it was silent.

I walked over the French doors and pulled back the heavy curtain to peek outside. The rain had stopped and the moon was now bright and full in the sky. Maine had some crazy weather. I started to take another sip of my water, when a movement stopped me. My heart stopped too. The figure moved through the garden. My first thought was to move away from the doorway, but instead I remained still, watching.

Within seconds, I recognized who it was. Dean. Probably leaving the pub for the night. It was nuts that I had just met the man, but I could already recognize his build and his walk, long, sure strides. Confident and manly. He headed toward the guest-house, only to pause. Then he changed direction and headed toward Jack's shed. He disappeared around the side of the build-ing, only to return a couple minutes later.

As he walked back toward the guesthouse, I stepped away from the door, letting the drape close more. I didn't want him to catch me watching him. He headed into his little cottage and I smiled. He'd checked on Jack again. He did believe me. Then my smile faded. And maybe he didn't think it was just someone goofing around.

"SO YOU ARE GOING to wait tables?" Oliver said, watching me as I pulled my hair up into a messy bun on the top of my head.

"Yeah, it sounded like it." I used my phone to check my hair. "Does this look okay? Maybe I should just put it in a ponytail."

"You look beautiful."

I smiled, appreciating his kind words. Didn't feel beautiful. I felt exhausted and stiff from spending the rest of the night sleeping in a chair. I couldn't bring myself to leave Oliver and go to one of the bedrooms. Who was I kidding? I was too scared. I had to get my nerves in check if I was going to live here. It wasn't like Oliver would be here forever.

"Soph, you're the boss. Shouldn't you be learning to run the place, not waiting tables?"

"I'm not going to be waiting tables all the time." At least I didn't think I would be. "I'm just helping out because Brady needed this afternoon off. As a boss, I'm sure I'll have to fill in wherever and whenever I'm needed."

Oliver shuddered dramatically. "Well, that sounds awful."

Oliver hated waiting tables. He refused to do the work that everyone associated with out-of-work actors. Fortunately, I had worked at a diner for a few months, so I at least knew what I was doing today. I probably shouldn't mention to Dean that I'd actually been fired from that job for spilling a glass of orange juice on a kid's head.

I adjusted my hair again, bringing up the camera on my phone to check it again.

Oliver stood up and came around the kitchen counter. He put his hands on my shoulders and forced me to look at him. "Soph, you just need to remember you can do this. You can."

I pulled in a deep, calming breath, then hugged him. "You're right. Today, my role is the new owner of Steamy's, who also happens to be helping out her staff by waiting tables. I've got this."

"You do."

I nodded with determination. "What are you going to do today?"

"I'm going to go explore the town."

My determination deflated. I would so much rather do that. No, I scolded myself, I was doing exactly what I moved here to do. And I'd have plenty of time to explore Friendship Harbor.

"Okay, scope out all the coolest places so we can check them out together later," I said, keeping my attitude positive.

"I will, and I'll feed Jack and let him out in his pen."

"Perfect," I gave him another hug, then straightened and held my hands out to my side. "How do I look?"

He assessed my plain, white tee shirt, black skinny jeans and hot pink Converse sneakers. "Ready to take on McSteamy and the world."

I smiled, then headed to the door, then called back, "And keep your ears open for any gossip about Cliff."

"You know I love some good gossip."

FIVE

AT THE BOTTOM of the stairs, I debated whether to go outside and enter the pub through the guest entrance or through the door that led to the pub's office and back room.

"I am the boss," I said aloud as if saying the words aloud would make me feel more confident. And actually, it seemed to work. I headed to the door that was paneled and painted white like most of the doors in the house.

I turned the doorknob, fully expecting it to be locked, but it turned easily in my hand. I peeked inside. The space was definitely an office with two wooden desks that had seen better days against two of the walls. On the desks were computers that looked as if they were purchased in the early 2000s. Gray boxy monitors and tower cases hummed loudly with tangled wires coming out of every port like they were on life support. Papers were stacked in messy piles and there were coffee cups filled with pens and other office supplies on each desk. I wandered over and picked up some of the papers placed there. Delivery invoices for food and alcohol. Other bills that had been marked with scrawling, male writing as paid. Dean's handwriting, I suspected.

Aside from that, the room was relatively bare. The white walls were devoid of any decorations, except for a round clock that reminded me of a school room clock and a dry erase board with the employees' upcoming shifts written in black. I walked over to it and saw all the employees I'd met already. Dean, Brandy, Chad, and Jimmy. There were a few other names. Dave, Janelle, and Marnie, but from the looks of their schedules, they were all part-time.

This space really needed some sprucing up. It was downright depressing, honestly. I would have to fix that. I started by picking up the red dry erase marker and drawing some flowers around the edge of the scheduling. Then I added some green stems and leaves. It seemed a waste not to use some of the other colors, after all. I stepped back, pleased with my work.

Then I added under the schedule in blue ink, "Team work makes the dream work." There. That was so much more inviting than just a plain, old schedule.

I moved to the open door on the other side of the room. It led into a storage area. This space was the polar opposite of the starkness I'd just seen. In fact, this was semi-organized chaos.

Boxes of liquors and beers lined one side of the room. On metal shelves, there were cans and boxes and bins of food supplies and drink mixers. There was extra glassware and dishes. Away from the food and drinks, in the corner were rags and brooms and mops resting in yellow industrial buckets.

In that same area were a line of lockers for the employees to store their personal items. I saw Brandy had labeled hers with a glittery name tag and some artwork that must have been made by her son. I smiled. I liked her right away, and this confirmed why. She was fun. She was positive.

"You're here."

I turned to see Dean in the doorway, all signs of the almost friendly guy from last night gone and replaced by the cool, unreadable dude I first met. Great. Not fun.

"I am here." I smiled, determined to stay positive. *I'll win you over yet, Surly McSteamy.*

"I'm not sure if it sets a good precedent for the boss to be late for her own shift."

I knew he was trying to put me in my place, but his words had the opposite effect. "You just called me boss." I grinned, but then looked appropriately contrite. After all, he was right. "But your point is taken. You're right. I won't be late again." To be fair, I hadn't even realized I was late, but I suspected bosses didn't make excuses either.

His emotionless expression slipped, a glimpse of irritation flashed in his golden eyes, then it was gone. He tossed me an apron, which I caught right before it fell to the ground. I shook it out, put the strap over my head and tied the strings around my waist.

"A four top just sat down by the window," he said, holding out an order pad and pitcher of water. I suppose I should be glad he didn't lob those at me too. "Please tell me you have actually waited tables before."

"I have," I said proudly.

"Of course you have. Isn't that the true profession of all actors?"

I managed a small laugh through my gritted teeth. I really wish I understood this guy. But I wasn't going to let him get to me. I was here to learn about the pub. Meet some of the locals.

And as tempted as I was to yank the pad and water out of his hands, I politely took them and headed in the direction he indicated with a bob of his head. The pub was relatively quiet. Just the one table and two other patrons seated at the bar. So it didn't seem like my tardiness was much of a problem.

Not thinking like a boss, I told myself. Every good boss starts by being a good worker. I smiled brightly and approached the table. The wooden table was seated by a group of women who all looked as if they were in their mid-thirties and clearly out for a girls' lunch. Their chatter and laughter helped me to feel less flustered.

"Hello, ladies, how are you today?"

The group fell silent, four sets of eyes roaming over me, and while not unfriendly, their perusal drove away what little peace I'd just gained.

"Are you the one with the killer llama?" one of them asked. The others waited expectantly for my answer.

I opened my mouth, then closed it, too caught off guard to know how to react. Finally, I managed. "Um, I do have a llama, but—"

"Knock it off, Michelle," a voice said from behind me. I turned to see a willowy blonde, who appeared to be about the same age as the women at the table, slip down from a barstool at the end of the bar and stroll toward me. Actually, it was more like a saunter, her hips swaying with each step. She stopped right beside me and glared at the table of friends. "You totally know that she inherited Sunny LaFleur's llama. Stop being so rude."

"I was just curious," the woman who was presumably Michelle said, raising a perfectly arched and tinted brow. One of the other women nodded.

"No, you were just being a trifling wench." The blonde hooked her arm through mine and led me away from the table back to the bar. Only to stop again, and look back at the table over her shoulder. "Oh, by the way, Michelle, you might want to ask Joe why his truck was parked outside Dawn Farrington's house again. I doubt she's getting her furnace serviced in August."

Michelle sputtered out an insult, and the foursome started talking again. This time there was no laughter.

"Th-thank you," I mumbled, not sure exactly what had just happened. But I quickly got the gist that this woman was someone who I didn't want to cross. There was a hardness in her blue eyes that belied her pretty smile.

"Happy to help. Especially with those witches. If you want to see who the mean girls turn into after high school, there they are. I'm Jessica, by the way." She offered me her hand, her fingers long and elegant and her nails perfectly manicured.

I accepted, noting that my own nails could use a little attention. "Sophie."

"Join me for a drink. I hate to drink alone." She gestured to the wooden stool beside her.

"Oh, I can't. Not while I'm working." As I said that, I saw Dean head toward the table of women, water glasses in hand.

"It looks like Dean has things under control. He usually does."

I didn't know what to make of that comment, but it did seem to be true.

"At least sit for a minute," she said again.

I hesitated, then perched on the edge of the stool. "Okay. Just for a minute."

Jessica smiled, then took a sip of the red wine in front of her. "I heard you just arrived in town. How do you like it so far?"

I made a face at that. "Well, it started out fantastic. For about an hour. Then poor Cliff and well...it seems like everyone knows about that already."

I expected her to brush my comment off, but instead she chuckled. "Rocky start for you or not, your arrival is the most excitement this boring, little town has had in years."

I made a face. "That's definitely a dubious honor."

She gave me a sympathetic smile. "You can't blame yourself. I heard Cliff's death was just a terrible accident. Unless something has changed?"

I shook my head. "No, that's what the sheriff believes. Just a freak accident."

"I wonder if Sheriff Pelletier will change his mind about that."

"Oh, I don't think so. He definitely thinks it's an open-and-shut case."

She studied me, her blue eyes searching. "And you don't believe that?"

"I—" Something told me to keep my doubts to myself. Since I didn't have any definitive proof that it was foul play, it was best not to share anything. "I can't imagine it could be anything but an awful accident. Did you know Cliff? He seemed like such a nice man."

Jessica nodded. "Everyone in town knew him, but I'm not sure 'nice' was necessarily the word most people used to describe him."

"Really?" I couldn't hide my curiosity. I wondered if she was going to tell me that same thing Dean had. That sweet, old Cliff was a player. Again, I had a hard time picturing the elderly, slightly stooped man as a womanizer. Although he did have that twinkle in his eyes, and he certainly was doing something to stay so jaunty.

"Oh, he was definitely a bit of a con artist. You know, didn't have any problems using people to get what he wanted." She lifted her glass and drained the rest of the red liquid.

"Really?" It seemed Cliff had quite the reputation. Goes to show you couldn't really know someone. Certainly not from meeting them for only an hour or so.

Just then, Dean appeared, setting another glass of wine in front of her. Their eyes met, although neither of them smiled. In fact, I saw a flash of dislike cross both of their faces. Dean walked away, disappearing into the kitchen. Interesting. What was their issue with each other? Although I was seriously starting to wonder if Dean liked anyone. Somehow, that idea made me feel a little better. Maybe it really wasn't just me.

"So I also heard you are an actress," she said after taking a sip of her new wine.

I smiled. "Was an actress. I've decided to take a break. Maybe permanently."

She sighed longingly. "I can't imagine ever wanting to leave a lifestyle like that. And to live in Hollywood." She shook her head. "I'd never leave."

I could see her in Hollywood. Long, blonde hair, beautiful skin with perfectly applied makeup. The nails. Even her clothing, a simple pale pink blouse and fitted, black, pencil skirt, looked expensive and very L.A. I thought of my own mother. Jessica was edgier, and of course younger, but both their vibes just oozed money.

A large diamond ring glittered on her finger. I noticed her fingernails again. Pale pink to match her shirt. Pale pink like the one Oliver discovered at Cliff's death site. But Jessica was not the type to wear press-on nails. I snickered silently. Oh no, she was on some manicurist's schedule for her bi-weekly appointment as we spoke.

"What do you do for a living?" I asked, expecting her to say lawyer or something equally professional.

She paused, her wine glass halfway to her rosy lips. "Oh, I do this and that. Mainly, I like to help people. I help a lot of the older people in town."

"Oh." I hadn't expected that. But maybe she came from money and just chose to help others because she'd been so fortunate. Or maybe there was money to be made in eldercare. The elderly were living longer and did need the help. But I really couldn't picture this woman, helping some old person prepare meals or get in and out of the tub. Although, I shouldn't really judge her just on looks. Look at what I was discovering about charming, old Cliff. And she had jumped in to help me. "That's really nice."

She nodded. "It's very rewarding."

Behind me, I heard the pub door open. "Well, I guess that's my sign to get back to work. But it was really great to meet you. I hope to see you again."

"Oh you'll see me. I rarely miss Tuesday, Two for One night. That's this town's idea of a wild time." She raised her glass as a goodbye.

Several people came in all at once, and I found myself busy. Thankfully, waiting tables was like riding a bike. Of course, I wasn't that great at riding a bike, either.

I didn't even notice when Jessica left, but I did notice when the table of busybody women left. And even though they didn't attempt to talk with me again, I was thankful when they were gone. Fortunately none of the other patrons felt the need to ask me awkward questions. I did notice a few curious looks, but I chose to believe that had more to do with a new face in the pub and less to do with Cliff's death. Even Dean, while back to his distant self, seemed to appreciate my help. I supposed that was basically friendly for him.

But my luck didn't last.

I heard the door open and glanced over to see an older woman, this short, white hair and a tall, thin frame, step into the pub. And right behind her was...oh no.

"Oh no," Karen said loudly as soon as she saw me. "I told you I didn't want to come here and I definitely do not want to if she's actually working here."

"Really, Karen? Really?" the older woman admonished in a low voice. She shot her a warning look, and to my surprise, Karen snapped her mouth shut and trailed behind her up to the bar. The older woman greeted Dean, and they started discussing something that I couldn't hear. I tried. Then gave up and I finished taking an order from a group of young guys, who'd clearly just gotten off work doing construction or other physical job, if their dusty clothes and the dirt under their nails were any indication. Again, I avoided the temptation to eavesdrop as I headed past the bar to put in the order. Or it might have been the stronger desire to avoid Karen's deadly stare.

"Jimmy," I called over the fans and fryers and tinny blare of oldies on an ancient boombox. "I need two seafood nachos and an order of extra-hot wings, please."

Jimmy grunted, which seemed to be his only form of communication.

"It's getting hot back here," I said, mainly to see if I could get any other response from him. Nope. Just another grunt. I shook my head, laughing to myself. Jimmy might be as tough to win over as Dean.

Still amused, I turned only to run straight into Dean, my body slamming against his and the top of my head bumping his chin.

"I'm sorry," I said, automatically reaching up to touch his jaw where I'd hit him. Our eyes met and his hand shot up to catch mine, moving it away from his face. Heat snaked up my neck to my cheeks, and I immediately felt awkward for doing something so personal. I stepped back, needing space between us.

He also took a step back too, but I was fairly certain it wasn't due to embarrassment and unwanted awareness. It was far more likely that he was concerned about further injuries.

"Sorry," I repeated.

"No worries. I actually came back here to talk with you."

Uh-oh. I wasn't sure what I'd done. In fact, things had been going pretty well. I only dropped one beer, which didn't even spill on anyone. And I might have dumped a cup of fish chowder on myself and had to get a new apron. I glanced down at myself at a still slightly visible splotch on my T-shirt. But they were both victimless crimes, so I was seeing my day as a success.

"Is everything okay? Did someone complain?"

"No," he said instantly. "You're doing fine. In fact, several people have mentioned they thought you were very nice."

I blinked, never expecting him to share a compliment with me. "I am nice."

"I never said you weren't. But you don't have to be right now."

I frowned. "I'm not following."

"Karen Grenier and her mother, Frances Robichaud, want to talk to you about having a 'celebration of life' gathering here after Cliff's funeral. And Karen is making it very clear she isn't exactly your biggest fan. Which I guess is understandable, given the circumstances. But I still don't think it's a good idea. She is not a nice woman on the best of days."

"Why, Dean, are you actually concerned for me?" I grinned.

A muscle in his jaw ticked for a moment, then he said gruffly, "I just don't think we need any more drama around here."

I nodded, still smiling, and I could tell from another twitch of his jaw that he knew I wasn't buying his excuse. Maybe there was a nice guy under all those muscles and brooding good looks.

"Well, I think it's the least I can do," I said.

"Why do I get the feeling you're going to do this for other

reasons?" Dean asked, his gaze narrowing. "You aren't still fixated on Cliff's death being more than an accident, are you?"

I shrugged, trying to play it cool. "I just think it's a nice idea."

And it was a perfect opportunity to talk to lots of people who knew Cliff. People who might know why someone would want to kill him. Plus, it really would be a nice gesture.

Dean looked as if he was reading my thoughts and he was unconvinced. "You do realize this is crazy? Just because you played an amateur detective on TV, doesn't mean you are one in real life."

His words shocked me. I should have been insulted that he was saying I couldn't solve a crime but mostly I was flattered. He'd seen my show? I couldn't contain another cheeky grin. "Dean, if you tell me you are a fan, I swear I don't think I'll know what to do. That's just too much charm for one afternoon."

I brushed past him to go talk with Frances Robichaud, but not before I heard him grumble something under his breath. Something that sounds suspiciously like a colorful expletive.

THE TWO WOMEN had moved from the bar to sit at a table nearby. Dean had given them drinks and menus, and they both looked up as I approached them. Karen glared, which I was beginning to think might be her only facial expression. But her mother smiled and extended her hand. Up close, I could see she was the older, kinder version of her daughter.

"You are most definitely Sunny LaFleur's granddaughter," she said, shaking her head. "It's like seeing a ghost."

I shook her hand and smiled back. "I've heard that before. You knew my grandmother well?"

"Oh yes, I was one of the witnesses at her wedding to your grandfather."

"Really?" I said, intrigued. "I have to admit, I haven't heard much about my grandfather." But of course, I hadn't heard much about my grandmother either.

Frances nodded, growing suddenly somber. "Well, that was messy business, so I'm not surprised."

What was messy business? But before I had a chance to ask what she meant, she gestured to one of the empty chairs. "Please sit down."

I did, still regarding her. Frankly, I was a little nervous to look at Karen. If looks could kill and all that.

"So, I'm sure Dean mentioned to you that I'm interested in having a celebration of life for Cliff here."

Out of the corner of my eyes, I saw Karen shift in her seat, her expression grim.

"Yes, he did."

"I know it's short notice," Frances said, also not looking at her daughter. "But this was one of his favorite places and I think it seems like the appropriate thing to do."

"Not that he ever did anything appropriate or otherwise for you," Karen muttered.

"Karen," Frances warned, shooting her a look only mothers could give. "He was your father."

Karen's lips pressed into a thin line. She leaned back in her chair and crossed her arms over her chest, clearly resigning herself to her mother's wishes. But one thing was very clear, Karen was not mourning her father. In fact, she seemed as angry as she had the first time I met her. What was the cause of all her hatred? And was it enough to do the old guy in?

"You'll have to excuse Karen's irritation with all of this," Frances said as if the other woman wasn't even there. "She and her father weren't always on the best of terms."

Clearly.

"And frankly, I wasn't always on the best of terms with him either, but I still believe he should have a proper memorial."

Karen's foot pumped up and down under the table as if she was just dying to give her opinion on all this, but she remained silent.

I nodded, pretending not to notice. "Of course. When is the funeral?"

"It will be on Wednesday evening. As of right now. I will let you know by tomorrow if anything changes."

I nodded, not sure what might change, but to be honest, I didn't know much about arranging a funeral. Maybe the funeral home might already be booked for another funeral. Did that happen? My grandmother requested not to have a service. So she was simply cremated.

I paused, a thought occurring to me. Maybe I should find out exactly where Grammy was now.

"Will Wednesday work?" Frances asked and I realized I hadn't said anything for a moment. *Stay focused here, Soph.*

"I'm sure we can work with you," I said, although I wasn't exactly sure about that either. This was my first day. I was just learning how to ring up food orders correctly. I definitely didn't know how to book a special event. Or if we normally even did special events.

Deciding my best course of action was to just be upfront, I said, "To be honest, I'm just learning about the pub and I'm not really sure how to go about arranging this."

Beside me Karen snorted. "You don't seem too sure about anything."

Frances shot her a warning look. I ignored her.

"So, let me send Dean back over to get an idea of how many to expect and what you would like served. But yes, we'd be honored to do this for you and for Cliff."

I excused myself, still not glancing at Karen as I went back to Dean.

"They want the celebration of life on Wednesday. Could you go over what they want with them?"

"Wednesday?" Dean said. "That's trivia night."

I gave him an incredulous look. "I think the trivia crowd will understand."

He looked doubtful, but sighed. "Okay." He dug around on the shelf under the cash register and found a small notebook and a pen. "Watch the bar."

I nodded, then saw another large group of about ten or twelve guys stroll in and take over the end of the bar. One of them waved to me and I took a deep breath. I'd never actually tended bar before but how hard could it be?

I was neck-deep in Miller Lites, Budweisers, and Jack and Cokes, when Brandy appeared beside me, already in her apron and ready to work. "Whoa, it looks like happy hour is in full swing today."

"Oh, thank God." I could have hugged the smiling blonde. "I lost track of who ordered what about six drinks ago."

"No problem, I know most of these guys' drinks by heart anyway. They are regulars." She took over filling several of the glasses I had lined on the mat in front of the beer taps.

"You can take off if you want," she said, picking up two pint glasses in each hand. "I'm here for the night, and Dave is here too. He's in the back, getting his apron. And Janelle is in at five."

Dave? Janelle? Oh right, I saw their names on the schedule in the office.

"I really appreciate you covering for me today," she called down the bar over the loud chatter of the patrons and the steady beat of the jukebox in the corner. "Ethan had a recital at the school and I hate leaving Dean on his own."

I assumed Ethan was her son.

"Of course. Are you sure you got this?"

She waved with a smile. "Absolutely."

I hesitated for a moment. I hated to leave if they still needed me, but as things were getting busier, I felt like I was more hindrance than a help. At least until I got more comfortable with the place. I started to take off my apron, then stopped. I had a couple tables that needed to be bussed and I'm sure there was some side work I could do to make the next shift easier.

I grabbed a large oval tray and headed to the first table.

"I truly don't understand why you are doing this, Mom?" I

heard Karen mutter to her mother. "That man did nothing but humiliate you for years."

"This isn't your decision," Frances replied, her voice quieter, the tone somewhere between determined and resigned. "There are plenty of people in this town who respected your father. Plenty who cared about him. And despite everything, it's just the right thing to do. We may have been separated for all these years, but legally and truthfully, in my heart, he was still my husband."

I paused, wiping down the table, listening closer. Frances and Cliff were still married?

"No, you weren't, Mom. He filed the divorce papers just before he died."

I shifted around the table, trying not to draw attention to myself. I wanted to hear this. Cliff filed for divorce just before he died. Was Karen talking just days before his death? Or literally just before he died?

I sneaked a quick glance at Frances, curious to see Frances's reaction to Karen's words. She didn't appear surprised by Karen's comment. Nor did she look pleased. If anything, she looked indifferent.

I focused on wiping the table again.

"Well, I'm still the only one he has to arrange something like this. And I plan to do it, only because it's the right thing to do. We're his only family here in town. And since I know you wouldn't do it, I will."

Karen leaned back in her seat, giving Frances a clearer view of me. I continued wiping, trying desperately to appear busy.

"Mom, if Dad was ever concerned about doing the right thing, he wouldn't have cheated on you. More than once."

My wiping paused. Wow, old Cliff was a dog.

"And," Karen continued, "he wouldn't have sued his own business partner and best friend. You and I both know Mac never deserved that lawsuit against him."

Mac? I needed to find out who Mac was.

"We've talked about all of these things before. I know your

father has hurt you, angered you, but we still have to do what's right," Frances insisted.

"Or what makes us look best," Karen said sarcastically.

Or maybe what makes them look the least guilty, I added silently.

"Hey."

I jumped, nearly knocking the dish-ladened tray off the table, but Dean, who'd spoken from beside me, caught it with only one knife hitting the floor with a clatter. I scrambled to snatch it up from the floor and put it back on the tray. From the corner of my eye, I could see both Frances and Karen were now watching me.

"Brandy told me you were heading out for the day," Dean said, taking the tray from the table before I could make another clumsy move.

"Yeah, I—I was," I managed, still feeling a little flustered and still feeling the two women's eyes on me. "I just wanted to finish clearing my tables."

"I got them," Dean said, and I wondered if he realized I was eavesdropping on Frances and Karen's conversation. I just hoped the two women didn't.

I wiped down the exceedingly clean table one last time, then headed to the back room to take off my apron. I debated introducing myself to Dave, but when I poked my head out into the pub, I saw a tall, twenty-something with a goatee and man-bun in a tie-dye, dark jeans and apron already talking to a large party near the windows.

Not wanting to interrupt him and not wanting to get any more critical looks from Dean, I decided to just leave through the office.

"Whoa," Oliver said as soon as I stepped into the kitchen. He was seated at the counter, drinking a can of soda and watching a video on his tablet. "It looks like you've had a day. Your hair is insane."

"It was actually pretty good," I said, although I did self-consciously touch my hair, but his reaction about my looks was quickly dismissed with my news. "But more than being good, it was also quite informative."

He set the soda down. "Oh yeah, do tell."

"Karen and her mother came into the pub and I overheard a lot of interesting tidbits from them." I shared what I'd heard, then waited for his reaction.

"So Cliff was an ass." Oliver shrugged. "This isn't really new information."

I gaped at him. "It also gives them plenty of reasons to want him dead. Karen hated him. Don't you remember she said something to the effect that I had no idea what I'd done when we were getting Jack? What did she mean?"

He considered from a moment, then shook his head. "I have no idea. What did she mean?"

"Well, I don't know either," I admitted, then reached for his soda and took a sip. "But it means something, right? It has to. That isn't something you randomly say, especially when you've just discovered your dad was killed."

"You do realize there are more sodas in the fridge." He took his away from me quite indignantly.

I went to retrieve one, still thinking about the women's conversation. I cracked a can of lemon-lime soda open and took a long sip. "And Frances has plenty of reasons to want Cliff dead. He cheated on her. He embarrassed her. He apparently finally filed for divorce. Why now after they'd been separated for so long?"

"Maybe he was planning to get married," Oliver suggested absently, his attention returning to the video he was watching.

"Yes," I said loudly, causing him to start. "That makes total sense."

He sighed and powered down his tablet, seeing that I wasn't going to stop my out loud analysis. "Okay, so maybe he was planning to get married. Why would his soon-to-be ex-wife plan his memorial?"

"Well, she said that herself to Karen. It's what family does."

"And it does deflect any suspicion. A woman wouldn't organize a celebration of life for an ex-husband who she hated enough to kill."

"Exactly," I agreed.

"But why kill him now? It sounds like she had years to do that."

"Maybe she knew she'd no longer inherit anything if the divorce was finalized."

"That does sound feasible," Oliver conceded. "Or maybe Karen killed him for the very same reason. She's clearly close to her mother. Maybe she did it to make sure her mother got what she thought she deserved for having such a terrible husband. Though if Cliff was planning to get remarried, wouldn't his new girlfriend be planning his funeral?"

"Maybe she is and Frances is just being defiant with this celebration of life."

"So she's just a catty cow despite the sweet appearance? I can buy that."

I nodded. "Okay, I'm going to jump in the shower and then we need to go."

"Go where?"

I paused in the doorway. "Did you happen to see the local library while you were exploring today?"

His less than thrilled expression was all the answer I needed.

"I'll be right down and then we are headed there."

"WOW, THIS STREET IS BEAUTIFUL," I said as we walked in the direction of the library. Pleasant Street ran perpendicular to Main Street where the pub was located. The quiet street was lined with huge old oak trees and large Victorian houses, both of which looked like they'd been there for a hundred years. The sun was low in the sky, casting shadows, but the air was warm. A group of young kids played on the lawn of one of the houses with a Frisbee. A small dog yapped on the front step of the house next door. We walked past another cross street until I spotted the library, a large white, clapboard building that looked as if it might have been a sea captain's house at one point. There were columns that framed either side of the front entrance and a widow's walk that adorned the roof. A sunroom made of multiple panes of glass jutted out of one side, and I could see sofas and computers through the windows.

"What a great building." I hurried up the walkway, afraid we might miss our chance to get in. It was already after five. And a Friday. But I was pleased the hours on the door said they were open until six.

"Maybe we should come back tomorrow. This is a small, older library. It might take us a long time to find whatever we are looking for," Oliver said, clearly dismayed the library was still open. "Did I mention there is a cute, little boardwalk with a couple restaurants right down on the waterfront? We could get lobster and a drink." He smiled hopefully.

"We are already here. Let's just take a look." I pushed the door open and stepped inside. The place was quiet, other than two ladies who worked at the front counter. The conversation stopped as soon as they saw us.

"Hi there," the one closest to us said with a warm smile. She was in her mid-fifties with salt-and-pepper hair pulled up into a tight bun. She wore a floral dress with a lace collar that looked like it could be from another time period. The other woman could have been about the same age, but her long, brown and caramel-high-lighted hair, glasses with funky frames and fashionable tunic made her seem much younger.

A good reminder that you are only as old as you feel. And clearly the one woman felt very young and very hip. I thought of my grammy, knowing she must have adhered to that philosophy.

"Can I help you?" the less hip lady asked.

"Yes," I said. "We wanted to look for some local news articles."

"Do you have a specific date or year?"

"No. Probably in the last ten years. Maybe twenty." That didn't exactly narrow things down.

"Well, if it's within the last twenty or so, we have completed digitizing those issues and you can search them on our database online. Anything before that is still on microfilm. Becky, could you show them to the computers."

The young fifty-something smiled, revealing deep dimples and an adorable smile. "Sure. Come right this way."

"So are you two here on vacation?" Becky asked as she led us down the main corridor of the library. "I haven't seen you here before."

"No, I actually just moved here, but Oliver is visiting. Helping me settle in." I have to admit I was a little pleased she didn't somehow already know I was the new person in town who'd let my supposedly deadly llama loose.

Unfortunately that pleasure only lasted for a second as Becky stopped. "Oh," she said, placing a hand on my arm, "you are Sunny LaFleur's granddaughter. I heard you had arrived."

She gave me a pained, sympathetic look, which was so sweet and sincere, it took away some of the disappointment of being the main topic of local gossip.

"Yes, news really travels fast in this town."

Becky nodded, her brown eyes behind her modern cat-eye glasses still very kind. "It does, but you know, most people don't believe the negative. I know I always take what I hear with a grain of salt. An accident is an accident."

I believed she was sincere. Of course, there I was trying to prove it wasn't an accident. That was ironic.

She continued on, directing us into the sunroom I'd seen from outside and to the bank of computers. "You can use any of these to look up our local papers. I'll let you do your thing." She started to leave the room, but paused again. "It was very nice to meet you. I know you will love it here." She smiled, then looked toward Oliver. "I love your hair. I was thinking of trying a fun color in my hair. I might just do it."

"You'd rock it," Oliver told her with an approving nod.

Beth grinned wider and disappeared back down the hall.

"I like her," he said. "You should be friends with her."

"I really should," I agreed wholeheartedly. She was much more my type of chick to hang out with than the savvy blonde Jessica I'd met at the pub.

I settled on a metal stool in front of one of the computers. Oliver pulled another one over and sat beside me.

"I have to admit I'm kind of disappointed we don't have to go through reels of microfilm in some dark basement," I said, jiggling the mouse to make the computer screen flicker to life. "Somehow that feels more covert and dangerous."

"Ack, no, that sounds awful," Oliver groaned. "Plus, you know I don't have the attention span for all that. And the only danger I like is wearing last year's fashions."

I laughed. "Rebel."

"You know it, baby." He looked around the room while I typed. "This room is actually really nice. Airy yet cozy." He turned his attention back to what I was typing. "Who is Mac again?"

I'd typed Cliff Robichaud and Mac into the search bar. "He was Cliff's business partner. Apparently Cliff and he got into some sort of dispute about the business and it ruined their friendship. I'm hoping to find some court records or something. But I don't have Mac's last name."

I hit search and several articles came up, including one from yesterday. I hesitated to click the link. But curiosity got the better of me. I moved the mouse and tapped it.

"Oh God," I moaned. A full, front-page article on Cliff's death. Including my name and Jack Kerouac's. "Well, this explains how everyone knows about me. I didn't even need word of mouth. Jack and I got actual press."

Oliver scanned the article. "At least they didn't get a quote from Karen."

I guess that was something.

I closed that article and began to read through the other links. Cliff appeared in the real estate reports. Often.

"Wow, Cliff must have had some real money after all these

land deals," Oliver said after we finished reading about yet another sale.

"But I don't see anything about him owning a business. And I don't see anything about a Mac. Maybe if we at least had a full first name, we could find something. What would Mac be short for?"

"Malcolm Porter," a raspy voice said from somewhere in the glass room. We both turned on our stool, scanning the room. Then we spotted her, an elderly woman, leaning forward to peer at us from a wingback chair several feet away from us.

"You're looking for Malcolm Porter."

SIX

"OH HELLO," I said after my initial shock passed. I stood and walked over to the elderly woman. "I didn't realize you were in here."

"Clearly. You do know this is a library. You are supposed to be quiet. But since I could hear everything you were talking about, I decided to help you out. It's hard to read when people are jabbering."

"I'm sorry," I said, noting the large-print novel laying on her lap. "We didn't mean to disturb you. I'm Sophie and this is my friend Oliver."

She snorted. "I know who you are. You saw your name was all over the front page of the paper. I guess I shouldn't be surprised. They say the apple doesn't fall far from the tree."

I frowned. What did she mean by that? I started to ask her, but she abruptly slammed her book shut and moved forward in her seat as if she was going to stand. Instead, she squinted around.

"I'm ready to go anyway, except my daughter has disappeared. She does that."

It wasn't hard to imagine why her daughter disappeared. This frail, almost skeletal woman exuded crotchety and difficult.

"Do you want me to see if I can find her for you?" I asked gently, hoping to soothe her bad temper just a bit.

"No, she'll be back." She scowled at me as if that was the stupidest offer she'd ever heard. I was starting to have some serious concerns about the false advertising of the name of this town.

"So you are looking for information about Cliff Robichaud, are you?" She pinned me with dark, shrewd eyes. Her body might be old and failing, but I could see her mind wasn't failing her in the least. And although she was rather intimidating, I could see she wanted to share what she knew about him.

I sat down in the chair next to hers. Oliver stayed on his stool, regarding the ancient woman warily.

"Yes, we were actually trying to find out some information about a business he owned with Mac. Um, I guess Malcolm Porter."

She nodded, leaning toward me. "Cliff did own a business with Mac. A seafood wholesale company. You know, a place that sells fresh seafood to other businesses around the area. They did a big business with the restaurants in Bar Harbor. Damned tourists can't get enough lobster. Those two men made some big money, peddling shellfish all up and down this area."

"So what happened?" I asked. "Why did they end such a successful business?"

"Cliff was always too greedy for his own good," the elderly woman said.

Greedy and a womanizer. Cliff's charming image was getting shadier by the minute.

"The way I heard it," the old woman said, leaning closer to me. "He and Mac agreed that they would open another such company farther down the coast to supply seafood to places like Rockport and Camden. So Mac took some of the money to purchase a new facility, and when he did, Cliff claimed he'd never agreed to such a thing and that Mac was trying to steal from him. He sued Mac, and somehow won. Well, that was the end of their business, but not before Cliff walked away with full ownership of the company. He sold it to some millionaire from Massachusetts. Massachusetts. Hmph." She said the last bit as if that was the ultimate sin of the whole tale.

She sighed and fell back in the chair as if sharing all that had exhausted her, but then she instantly found her second wind and straightened up again. "Mac ended up with virtually nothing. No business, no equity in the company and a huge black mark on his reputation. As you can imagine, there was no good blood between those two after that."

Yes, that definitely sounded like a situation that would cause a lot of anger and resentment between the two men. And frankly, it sounded like a very possible reason for Mac to want Cliff dead.

"Of course, there were folks in town who believed Cliff's account of everything. He was wily like that. He could convince just about anyone just about anything he wanted. I was friends with his dearly departed mother. She was a good woman. A straightforward woman. And even she said she'd never been able to punish him as a child, because he could sweet-talk himself out of any mess." She shook her head in dismay as if imagining what raising a child like that must have been like.

From what I was learning, it seemed more and more like someone finally gave him the ultimate punishment.

"Mom." A woman who appeared to be in her sixties entered the sunroom. This was the missing daughter, obviously, although if I hadn't heard her call to her mom, I wouldn't have guessed they were related. Where the elderly woman in the chair was thin and angular, her daughter was soft and round. Her figure was full, but her face was sweet and quite pretty. I imagined in her youth, she was probably quite stunning. Whereas her mother looked like she would have always been hard and somewhat masculine.

I stood up immediately and greeted her with a smile. "Hi there, I'm Sophie LaFleur."

The new woman hesitated before taking my hand almost as if she really didn't want to touch me. But after a second, she did. I was surprised to feel the roughness of her hands, which didn't seem to correlate with the softness of the rest of her. Oliver joined me, also offering his hand, and I noticed she didn't seem to have the same hesitation with him as she did with me.

"I'm Millie Hall, and this is my mother, Eleanor."

"These kids were asking me about that awful Cliff Robichaud," her mother said, her raspy voice dripping with dislike.

"Mom," she scolded softly. "It isn't kind to speak ill of the dead."

Eleanor made a noise again and sank back in her chair. "When he was alive you said not to gossip. Now he's dead and I can't speak the truth? If you're a lousy person, you're lousy."

"You'll have to forgive my mother," Millie said as if she'd said that exact phrase many times before. Which I had no doubt she had. "She can get caught up in the idle gossip that goes around this town. I've always found Cliff to be a very nice man."

"So you knew him well?" Oliver asked.

"No," she said quickly, almost too quickly. "No, not well. But what I did know of him, I found to be..." She shook her head slightly as if searching for the right word. "I found him to be quite decent." For a moment, I thought I saw her pale blue eyes, also nothing like her mother's, cloud with tears.

Behind her, Eleanor snorted.

I looked at the ancient woman, waiting for her to add more, but apparently the scoffing noise was all she needed to say. When I looked back to Millie, her eyes were no longer watery.

Millie sighed, a deep sound like that of utter exasperation and exhaustion, but her voice was soft and tolerant as she turned to her crusty, old mother and said, "Let me help you up, Mom. We should head home. It's almost time for Wheel of Fortune."

She moved to help her skeletal mother to her feet. Then she held out a black cane to her. The cane had a crooked handle and was stabilized with four small feet attached at the bottom that reminded me of the legs of some weird insect. The ancient woman snatched the cane from her. Eleanor didn't utter a word of thanks as she was balanced on her black, orthopedic shoes and began tottering past us. Then she stopped and pointed at the chair with her cane. "Don't forget my book."

Obediently, Millie got the book from where it must have slipped off Eleanor's lap when she stood.

"It was nice to meet you," Millie said, taking her mother's elbow and leading the stooped, shuffling woman from the room.

Eleanor said nothing.

"Wow, there's a mother who could give Joan Crawford a run for her money," Oliver muttered as soon as they were out of earshot. "Millie, you better hide all the metal hangers."

I gave him a disapproving look, although I didn't actually disagree. Eleanor was terrifying.

"Well, she certainly hated Cliff, that's for sure."

"Oh yeah, she couldn't wait to start throwing shade on him. But there is no way she could have killed him. She'd still be shuffling her way to where he was killed as we speak."

"True." I nodded. "What about Millie?"

"I think that poor woman suffers PTSD from dealing with her mother," he said dryly. "But I can't imagine her hurting anyone, much less killing them."

"Did you notice she looked almost teary when she talked about Cliff? Doesn't that seem like a weird reaction to have about someone you say you didn't really know?"

Oliver shrugged. "You get teary every time Augustus dies in Fault in our Stars, and he's a fictional character."

"That is a sad movie," I said. "And you get teary too."

He shrugged, not denying it.

"Well, if there is one thing I'm quickly learning during this whole experience, it's the fact that you can't really judge anyone on first impressions."

"Except Karen."

"Yeah, except Karen." That was one woman who did not inherit her father's charm.

"Let's go down to the boardwalk and get lobster," Oliver

suggested, clearly done with detective work for the night. "I recently heard damned tourists love lobster."

I HAD to admit it was nice to simply go out and have something to eat with Oliver and not think about Cliff or potential murder for just a while. The small boardwalk was as quaint as Oliver had promised, lined with a few shops, a small arcade, and a restaurant that looked out over the harbor. I also discovered why tourists loved lobster.

I groaned as we walked back to the house. "I'm stuffed. All that butter and deliciousness. I think I might have to eat lobster every day."

"And don't forget those clams at the pub. Those are dangerous. I'd weigh three hundred pounds if I stayed here," Oliver said, blowing out his lips to illustrate his overweight, clam-filled self.

I laughed, then fell silent as we walked along Water Street. The sun had disappeared below the horizon while we'd been sitting outside enjoying our lobster and wine. But I could still hear the crash of the ocean and smell its saltiness in the cool air. Warm light shone from the windows of all the gorgeous, old houses, lining the street.

"This place is really very cool," Oliver said, reading my thoughts.

It was. Despite all the craziness of the past couple days and the few grouchy people I'd encountered, I had to admit I was falling in love with Friendship Harbor. Suddenly, I wished I could speak to my grandmother and tell her how thankful I was for all this.

We turned up Main Street, walking slowly, stopping to look in the windows of the shops. Most of the places were open, summer hours for the tourists. Quite a few people roamed the street, enjoying the late summer evening like we were, but there was still such a peacefulness that just couldn't be found in L.A.

I stopped to admire some handmade pottery in one of the store-fronts, when I spotted a decorative llama doll of wool and sticks.

"We should probably head back and check on Jack," I said, suddenly feeling guilty. "He's got to be lonely. I've been gone all day."

"I hung out with him for a while today," Oliver said. "He does like company. So I showed him some llama videos on YouTube and we hung out in the sun for about an hour."

"Aww." I smiled appreciatively. "You are falling in love with Jack too."

"I'm just trying to stay on his good side. I saw the damage that beast can do."

When he saw my stricken expression, he immediately clarified. "Not his possible deadly kicking ability. I was talking about when he spit on Karen."

I sighed with relief. I didn't want my best friend in the Killer Jack camp. Then despite myself, I laughed. "He really does have amazing aim."

"And her face," he said, laughing too. "That was priceless."

We were still chuckling when we reached the house and headed around the back to Jack's pen. I could see the white fur of the llama, glowing in the back porch light. He stood at the fence as if he was waiting for us.

"Did you leave Jack out when we left?"

Oliver shook his head. "No. I definitely put him back in his stall. He gave me attitude the whole time, because he'd found a particularly delicious patch of clover."

"I'm starting to think he should have been named Houdini instead of Jack Kerouac."

I started across the lawn, when I saw it. The shadowy figure I'd seen last night. But this time the figure was inside the pen with Jack.

"Hey," I yelled, feeling a bit more emboldened having Oliver with me. "What are you doing?"

The figure turned toward us, and unlike the night before I could make out part of a face, although the person again wore a hood that shielded most of their features. But I had to admit I was relieved to see it was an actual person. In the wee hours of last night, I had started to let my mind mess with me, imagining the figure was a ghost. A dark spirit lurking out here, waiting to get me.

But now I could see the shape was clearly a human, and a smaller human at that. That realization made me even braver. I did take kickboxing lessons as prep for a scene in Murder, She Texted where Jennifer got training from a gym in exchange for solving the murder of a beloved instructor. The man had been crushed to death by a weight bag.

"Who are you?" I called to the petite person, rushing toward the paddock.

The person looked wildly around as if trying to find the best way to escape, but to my surprise, he or she didn't run.

"Who are you?" I demanded when I reached the gate and the person was mere feet away from me.

The person looked down at the ground, remaining still, shoulders slumping in defeat. After a moment, the hooded figure looked up, and I could see young, pixie-like features clearly. It was definitely a she. A young she.

The girl tugged at the hood of her sweatshirt to reveal long, strawberry blonde hair, pale skin, a small, upturned nose, and tear-filled blue eyes.

"I'm sorry," she said, her voice wobbling. "I was just coming to see Jack, and he got out of his stall. I was trying to get him back inside."

"It's okay," I said, immediately moved by her distress. "Really, it's okay."

More tears rolled down her face. "I just wanted to make sure he's okay."

"Of course, he's okay," I reassured her.

She sobbed harder. This really wasn't going well at all. What had her so upset?

Carefully, I opened the gate and stepped inside, still leaving space between myself and her. Jack came over to sniff my hair, then wandered over to sniff the teenager. She rubbed his woolly head, although that didn't seem to calm her either.

"What's your name?" I asked gently.

"Hannah," she managed between hiccups. "Hannah Quinn."

"Hi, Hannah, I'm Sophie and this is Oliver." I gestured to my friend.

Oliver smiled warmly at her. "Don't be so upset, he gave me fits earlier trying to get him back into his stall. He can be super stubborn when he wants to be."

His reassuring words only triggered a new wave of tears from the girl.

Oliver shot me a dismayed look.

"Why are you so upset?" I asked, moving a little closer. She didn't move away, which I took as a good sign.

She looked down, her fingers still curled in Jack's woolly curls. I could see she was still struggling with her tears. My first instinct was to hug that poor girl, but I didn't want to freak her out any more than she already was. She poked the ground with the tip of her pink Converse, and just when I thought I was going to have to prompt her again to talk to me, she pulled in a deep breath.

"I'm the one who let out Jack that day," she blurted out, her admission followed by a new wave of tears.

Or course, I knew what day she was talking about.

"Oh," I said, trying to find the right thing to say. "Did you do it on purpose? Why?"

"No! Of course not!"

That was a relief. "So it was an accident. That's okay, then."

"No, it's not. I let Jack out and now someone is dead and the police are going to take Jack away. Maybe even put him down."

I frowned. What? The police were planning to confiscate my llama? Put him down? Over my dead body. Jack wasn't going to be punished or killed for something he didn't even do. Though I couldn't exactly tell Hannah that. She looked like she was thirteen years old at most.

"Why would you think that?" Oliver asked softly, joining us in Jack's pen.

"That's what they do, right?" Hannah said, between sniffles. "Like when a dog bites someone and they make the owner put it down."

I let out a sigh of relief. She was just worried about that happening. She didn't have any proof it would. Although her reasoning did make sense. And who knows what nasty Karen could push the police to do. Again, she reminded me of the Wicked Witch of the West. *I'll get you, my pretty, and your spitting llama too.*

"You don't have to worry about that," I assured her, and to some extent, myself. "Sheriff Pelletier wouldn't take away Jack. He knows if Jack did kick Cliff Robichaud it was an accident."

For the first time, the teenager looked hopeful. "Do you really think so?"

I nodded adamantly. "Yes. He told me so."

That wasn't quite true, but I did think Sheriff Pelletier seemed like a nice, rational guy, who wouldn't see a llama hurt. Maybe there were rules though. Laws against deadly camelids. It was a thought that hadn't crossed my mind until now and I didn't like it. But I had to assume if they were treating Jack as a harmful creature, they would have already come to take him to the gallows.

Unfortunately my reassurance only calmed her for a moment, then more tears threatened to spill down her cheeks. "I'm so glad Jack is safe, but the accident was still my fault. I came over after summer camp to give him a treat and I must have left the gate open. I was in a rush to get to my friend's house because we were going to the movies. I brought Jack some Froot Loops. Miss Sunny said it was okay. But I know I must not have locked the gate right."

She crumbled into tears again.

"Jack likes Froot Loops?" I asked, hoping to distract her. I knew exactly how she felt. It was a lot of burden to believe you were the cause of a person's death. Accident or not. "See, I'm so glad you came over here. I would have never known Jack liked those."

She nodded, swiping at her face to wipe away the flood of tears. She sniffed. "He also likes Honey Smacks."

"He's got good taste. I like those too." I moved forward to touch the girl's arm. I was prepared for her to pull away, since she didn't know me and she might find it awkward, but she didn't. Instead she offered me a wobbly smile, which melted my heart. She reminded me of myself at her age with her red hair and freckles.

"You know," I said, wanting to comfort her further, "I think you are very brave to admit all this to me. You made a mistake and you were awesome enough to own it. A lot of people wouldn't do that."

She considered my words for a moment, then sighed. "Thanks. But I still feel like total garbage."

I understood that very well. But she certainly shouldn't feel any responsibility in Cliff's death, especially since I was growing more and more certain that Jack hadn't been to blame.

"Do you happen to remember when you would have been here that day?" I hated to freak her out more with questions, but in the end, it would make her feel better. I was sure of that. I planned to have her totally off the hook, once the truth came out about Cliff's death being a murder.

Hannah thought for a moment. "It had to have been around two-thirty. I came to give him a handful of Froot Loops. I never give him more because Miss Sunny said too much sugar isn't good for him. Then, I left. The movie started at three and I was afraid I was going to be late."

I considered her timeline. I was certain Cliff left here around one. And when the officer came to notify me about Jack being loose, it was around three. That would mean within a half an hour time span, Jack would have had to have gotten to the scenic walk, kicked Cliff, someone discovered his body, called the police, and for the police to arrive, and the body to have been taken away by three fifteen or so. That didn't make sense.

Of course, I wasn't about to go over all of this with a teenager. And right now, it was more important to assure Hannah that I wasn't upset and Jack wasn't at risk of being taken away by the police.

"You know what?" I said brightly.

She blinked, clearly confused by my sudden cheerful shift. "No."

"I think you should come see Jack every day, if you can. He's been lonely since my grandmother passed away. And he's just getting to know Oliver and me. I know he likes seeing a familiar face."

Her eyes narrowed, and I could tell she still didn't know what to make of me.

"I really do need the help," I assured her. "And I'd even be willing to pay you if you help feed him, maybe help me clean out his stall, that sort of thing." Because I wasn't sure I was quite ready for all of that. Not several times a day, anyway.

Hannah gaped at me, but I was glad to see her wide blue eyes were no longer filled with tears. "You'd pay me to help out with Jack? Even after it was my fault he got loose? I can tell you're not from Maine."

I wasn't sure what that meant, exactly. Maybe she had preconceived notions about Californians. But I gave her another smile. "Of course. I really do need help with him. And the gate was an accident. How would a hundred bucks a week sound?"

She finally smiled. Grinned, actually. "Shut up. A hundred bucks? That would be amazing! I'll never leave the gate open again, I swear."

"I know you won't." I held out my hand. "So we have a deal?"

She took it without hesitation. "Yes." She shook my hand, then turned to hug Jack around the neck. Jack's long lashes lowered in what looked like a llama version of an eye roll, but he allowed the snuggle.

"I think I got the best deal," Hannah said, mainly to Jack. Then she released him and gave me a huge smile. "I'll be over tomorrow after summer camp. I have to tell my mom."

She hurried out of the gate, only stopping to make sure it was closed and locked. "Thank you." She ran down the edge of the fence, disappearing into the trees like she'd done the first time I'd spotted her.

"No, thank you," Oliver said wryly as if Hannah was still standing here to hear him. "Way to get hired help to clean up after your llama."

I shot him an innocent look. "I was just trying to cheer her up."

Oliver shook his head. "I never knew you were such an opportunist."

"What?" I gave him an innocent look. "I only gave Hannah the opportunity to be around Jack, and Jack the opportunity to have some company and some Froot Loops."

"Mm-hmm." He wasn't buying my guilelessness for a moment.

"Okay," I admitted. "And maybe I did like the idea of not having to clean up Jack poops."

"Very savvy."

I curtsied.

"But I think the kid raked you over the coals. Did you see her reaction? I think you offered L.A. rates in small-town Maine. So maybe savvy isn't the right word."

He might have a point. "I wasn't going to negotiate with a kid who is probably barely a teenager." I clicked my tongue at Jack as if he was a horse. "Come on, Mr. Kerouac. It's time for some dinner and then sleep." I started toward the shed.

The llama lifted his head as if he was sniffing the air, probably trying to get a whiff of some more fruity goodness. But once he realized Hannah and her treats were gone, he ambled after me. Much to my surprise and relief.

"So speaking of opportunity," I said to Oliver as I shoveled some hay into Jack's stall. "Don't you think there is something wonky about the timeline the day of Cliff's death?"

I expected Oliver to disagree, or at least not be particularly suspicious of it, but to my surprise, he nodded. "It does seem to be off."

"I know, right? It seems like Jack would have had to have made his grand escape after Cliff was already dead."

Again, Oliver nodded. "It does seem like an awful lot would have happened in a pretty short amount of time."

"Exactly. And now that I think about it, even the puddle of blood where Cliff's body had been seemed pretty dried up."

Oliver looked less convinced about that observation. "I'm not sure about that. I mean what do we know about how fast blood absorbs into the ground?"

"Well, in season one, episode ten of Murder, She Texted, there was a murder on the beach and the director was getting frustrated with the prop guy because the blood looked too fresh. He wanted it to look like it had been there for a while. But it wouldn't absorb into the sand as quickly as he wanted."

"Umm, yeah, but that was fake blood. Who knows how real blood absorbs."

"I don't know. I mean fake blood is pretty realistic these days."

Oliver still didn't look convinced. He turned on the spigot to the hose used to fill Jack's water pail.

"Okay," I conceded. "Maybe we can't be totally sure about the blood thing, but the timeline still doesn't make any sense."

He dragged the hose over and began filling the water bucket. "I do agree on that one. So where do we go from here, Miss Detective?"

I sighed, giving Jack one last pet, before leaving and locking the stall door. Oliver turned off the hose. "I don't know. We don't even know for sure who found the body."

"You don't think it was Karen?"

I shrugged. "I assumed it was Karen. But maybe it wasn't."

"Karen seems like a stone-cold killer to me," Oliver said, looking down at his hands, dirty from the hose. He hesitated, then wiped them off on an old rag hanging on a nail over the spigot. He grimaced. "We need to order some hand towels for this shed. These rags are disgusting."

"I could ask Sheriff Pelletier who found Cliff." Although I

didn't really want to call him up and ask. He thought this whole situation was already closed, and I was pretty sure he wouldn't like me stepping on his toes by implying it wasn't.

"And what about Karen's mother? And this Mac guy?"

I did have a lot more people that needed to be looked into. I even wanted to know more about Millie Hall. Her reaction when I brought up Cliff did seem odd.

"Maybe I can find out more at the 'celebration of life' gathering. They probably will all be there."

Oliver nodded. "That's true. Or you could just meet more people who had a reason to want old Cliff bumped off."

I couldn't argue that. It seemed like just about everyone in this town had some reason to want Cliff Robichaud dead.

SEVEN

"I JUST CANNOT BELIEVE you are going to stay in that back-woods little town."

I sighed into my cell phone, just imagining my mother's appalled expression. "Mom, this town is beautiful and I wouldn't exactly call it backwoods. You make it sound like I'm in the middle of nowhere with no neighbors for miles around."

I dropped onto the window seat of the room I'd chosen as my bedroom. Since I discovered Hannah was my mysterious nighttime stalker, I decided I could actually stop sleeping on the sofa. I couldn't quite bring myself to use my grandmother's room. It still felt like her space and it seemed somehow impolite to intrude on it. Plus, I liked the coziness of this room with its slanted walls under the eaves with its lilac-covered wallpaper in purples and pinks.

"Well, there is no decent shopping for miles around. And certainly no Starbucks." I could practically see my mother's shudder through the phone.

"There are plenty of shops. I actually saw this one place that has the coolest pottery."

"Oh God, pottery. Next you'll be telling me you bought a quilt. Or even more ridiculous, made one."

I glanced at the quilt on the bed, made up of squares that

matched the walls. Well, I hadn't bought it, so that was something, right?

"Mom, you told me it was time to do something with my life. And I am."

"Your father and I meant a real job. You went from acting to running a pub. How's that any different than trying to be an actress and waiting tables here in L.A.?"

Her words stung a little. "It's a lot different. I own the pub. And I own this house."

"That house," Mom groaned. "That ancient cluttered house. I can only imagine how much junk my mother added over the years since I was last there."

I couldn't imagine my mother growing up here. My mother's style had always been clean, minimalist and modern. I suspected I was the only preschooler in the US who had an all-white, mid-century modern playroom.

"She has a lot of pretty amazing stuff," I said defensively, mainly because I really liked the things my grammy had collected. They were interesting. They were personal unlike the houses I grew up in. Everything had a story. "Did you know that Grammy was on the cover of the Woodstock album?"

I'd discovered the album cover framed in one of the other bedrooms, a blurry figure circled with her name and an arrow handwritten over it.

"You mean the person you can't even make out, sprawled on the ground, covered with a dirty blanket and surrounded by litter?"

I loved my mom, but sometimes she really did get on my nerves.

"I think it's pretty awesome she was there. And on the album cover too."

"Who even knows if that's really her," she scoffed. "Your grandmother never let the truth get in the way of a good story."

I really didn't want to argue. After all, I didn't know my grandmother, at least not in person, even though being here the past few days, exploring her home had made me feel close to her. But clearly, something had happened between her and both her daughters that had affected their relationship permanently. In fact, something had happened that seemed to have affected the locals too. I hesitated to ask my next question, not sure if I wanted to work Mom up any more than she already was. But my curiosity got the better of me. It usually did.

"Speaking of good stories, a couple of the locals have made comments to me about Grammy. One mentioned 'messy business' and another said that I didn't fall far from the tree. Do you have any idea what they might have meant?"

There was silence on the other end of the line, then she said, "Why on earth would someone say you didn't fall far from the tree? You are not a thing like my mother."

I wasn't so sure of that. Being in her house, surrounded by her things, I definitely did feel a connection with her. I felt like I was probably more like Grammy than I was my mother. Not that I'd ever tell Mom that. She still had hopes I'd be organized, immaculate, and aware of what designers were trending. I looked down at my old leggings and vintage AC/DC shirt and knew one hundred percent that would never happen.

"Well?" my mother prompted.

"It might have been because I was on the front page of the local paper. Because my llama accidentally killed someone. Well, he didn't actually kill anyone. It's just most of the town thinks he did. But I know he didn't."

There was more silence. "You have a llama?"

I tried not to laugh. That was the one thing she took away from that? I should have guessed the idea that I had a pet would overshadow the whole "someone died" portion of my story.

"Yes, Grammy had a llama. His name is Jack Kerouac."

There was a long-suffering sigh, then she said, "Of course, she did, and of course, he is."

"He's actually a really sweet llama," I said, feeling the need to defend him.

"I'm sure he is. When he's not killing someone."

I gritted my teeth. "I told you he didn't actually kill anyone."

She sighed, and I got the feeling she might be gritting her teeth too. "Alright, I'll take your word for it. Listen, it sounds like things are less than ideal there. I'm sure you could get enough from that place to buy a small condo back here. Your father and I would help you go back to college and get a degree that would be more useful than your theater degree."

I closed my eyes and pulled in a calming breath, determined not to overreact to her one of her favorite laments, my useless college degree. It hadn't been useless. I had worked as an actress for five years.

"Mom, I'm staying here," I said, firm, but calm. "I like it. This is really good for me."

Another pause followed by a sigh. "Okay. But I think I should come see you soon."

I loved my mom, but I definitely wasn't ready for a visit. Especially not in the middle of my murder investigation. If she thought my acting was crazy, she'd consider me certifiable for attempting to solve a murder. No, I was not going to mention that part of my arrival here.

"Sure, it would be great if you came to visit," I managed to say with feigned enthusiasm. "But I'm working a lot. Maybe you should wait until I get the swing of things with the pub. I mean, I am working a lot."

"Well, that's good, I guess," Mom said begrudgingly.

Yes, it would be good, if it were true. But in reality, I was still just working a short shift each day, only waiting tables. Even though I had asked Dean repeatedly to go over more of the daily running of the pub with me. Things like ordering and making schedules and doing payroll. Somehow, he always managed to make it sound like he would, only to tell me he didn't really have time. But that he would.

He wasn't going to, but I was not a confrontational person. I didn't really want to tick off the man who lived in my backyard and ran my business.

"It is good," I lied. "Really good. Great. Fabulous. Amazing." I clapped my mouth shut. I was overselling it.

"Okay, well, your father will be glad to know things are going fine there. For the most part."

Yes, for the most part.

"But now I need to dash. I have an appointment to show Ellen DeGeneres's stylist a condo in the Valley. Not one of my biggest sales, but who knows maybe she'll recommend me to Ellen."

"Wow, that would be awesome. I hope it goes great. I'll call you later this week."

"Okay, hon. I love you."

"Love you too, Mom." I tapped the cell screen to hang up. I leaned back against the pillows of the window seat. I did miss my mom, but I knew I dodged a bullet about her coming here. I needed to have the situation with the pub more under control. I needed to feel more established. And I need to solve the mystery of what happened to Cliff.

Then I could take on Mom.

Downstairs, I heard Oliver singing along with The Beatles. I regrouped for a moment longer, repeating my favorite quote about my mom. "There is no way to be a perfect mom, but there are a million ways to be a good one." I had to remember my mom, and my dad, only wanted the best for me.

I smiled, suddenly glad I talked to her. After all, her talk was only going to push me harder to make my life here work. See, moms did work in mysterious ways. Although it didn't go unnoticed that Mom had managed to avoid my question about the odd things some of the locals had said about Grammy. Something was not quite right there.

Oliver belted out the lyrics to Here Comes the Sun, off-key but definitely enthusiastic, and I decided I'd better go downstairs to see what he was doing. When I walked into the living room, Oliver was sitting on the floor surrounded by albums.

"Your grandmother has an amazing collection of vinyl," he said as soon as he saw me. He held up a copy of The Beatles' Abbey Road. "I bet some of these are worth money."

I shrugged. "Maybe. I know nothing about record albums."

While I loved all the oldies, I had no idea what they might be worth. Until moving into her house, I only ever played music through my phone or tablet. "They look really cool though."

Oliver nodded, looking through a few other covers before glancing back up at me. "So were you talking to Momma Leah?"

"Yes, she's on a campaign for me to come back to California, of course."

"Of course."

"And she wanted to come visit pretty much as soon as possible."

Oliver winced. "I hope you talked her out of that one. I love Momma Leah, but she is a lot. And that's saying something for me." He gestured down at himself in his purple jeans and hot pink T-shirt.

I smiled. "Yes, that is, although I find it easier to appreciate your 'a lot.'"

Oliver was one of my acting friends that my mother actually liked. Probably because at one point in his life he'd been a huge success. Of course, I always believed he'd be a success again. He just hadn't found the right part in my opinion. Nor was he really putting much effort into it.

I glanced at the old cuckoo clock hanging beside the doorway to the kitchen. "I suppose I better get showered and ready."

Cliff's funeral was that day at four o'clock.

Oliver started to pick up the albums, putting them back in the cabinet under a record player that looked like something from the seventies. "I'm dreading this. I don't think I've ever seen a real dead person."

I hadn't either. Definitely not a pleasant prospect. "I'm not thrilled with that either. But we will pay our respects, then get to work talking to people who might know more about Cliff. I'm hoping Mac Porter will be there."

"Do you think a man who clearly didn't have any love for Cliff would bother to go to his funeral?"

I shrugged. "I don't know. I'm banking on this being a small town, so everyone will be there."

"You're probably right," he said as he got to his feet. "After all, death by llama is bound to draw a crowd."

I shot him a dirty look. "I'm going to clear Jack's name."

He laughed. "The champion of falsely accused llamas. That's my friend."

AS WE WALKED up to the white, steepled church that looked like something out of a photo book of perfect New England images, I got the feeling my hunch was right. Large crowds of people in somber black clustered around the front lawn and along the walkway, while a long line waited to file in through the open double doors.

"Wow, he got a huge turnout."

I nodded. "Now we just have to figure out if Mac Porter is here."

Oliver looked dubious. "It would be easier if everyone had name tags."

I couldn't disagree. This was a lot of people, although I did already recognize quite a few faces from my time working at the pub.

"Sophie," a female voice called. I noticed several people looked in my direction. Apparently I did not need a name tag.

I turned to see Jessica Grace approaching, looking like a Hollywood bombshell in her tight, black, wiggle dress, plenty of cleavage and leg showing. And I had questioned the appropriateness of my sleeveless, black jumpsuit. The deep V-neck of my top suddenly seemed pretty tame. Then again, my lack of cleavage might have a lot to do with that. Jessica wasn't lacking on any curves. And she wasn't hesitating on whether to show them.

She strolled up to us, gliding smoothly in her six-inch heels, even on the grass. "Hi there. This is quite a crowd, isn't it?"

"Yes," I said, not sure what else to add. This was definitely not the typical funeral. Or at least I suspected it wasn't, so I gestured to Oliver. "Jessica, this is my friend Oliver."

"Oh, I know who he is. I'm not so old that I don't remember The High Jinx of Hayley and Jake." She held out her hand, that huge diamond of hers sparkling brightly on her extended fingers. "It's a real pleasure to meet you. Imagine, a real celebrity in our little town."

I guess she never saw my show, since she made no mention of me being a celebrity. Of course, my show had mainly done best in the forty-and-above demographic.

Oliver took her hand. "Nice to meet you."

Jessica smiled, and I'm pretty sure a starving crocodile looked less predatory. "It's more than nice to meet you."

He flicked a quick look at me, then managed to disengage his hand from hers. If she sensed any discomfit from him, she didn't show it.

Jessica studied Oliver for a moment longer, then cast a look around the crowded church lawn. "Cliff certainly got a big turnout. Amazing for someone who had so many enemies."

"Did he really have that many people who disliked him?" I asked, not exactly pleased. I already had a handful of possible killers. It might take years to investigate half the town.

"Well, Cliff was either loved or hated. But I guess the good people of Friendship Harbor are overlooking most of his shady behavior today. Funny how death will do that."

I nodded, scanning the crowd. People did look appropriately somber. Then my gaze landed on a tall, burly man with a graying beard. Although I couldn't hear him from this distance, the movement of his hands and the flash of anger in his eyes made it clear he was agitated. Then noticed who he was talking with. Frances Robichaud.

"Check out Millie Hall," Jessica said, drawing my attention back to her.

"I'm sorry," I said, still half watching the large man's erratic motions. "Who?"

"Millie Hall?" Jessica said, tipping her head in the direction of the short, portly woman we'd met at the library. "You probably haven't met her. She usually isn't far from her mother's side. I've helped them out over the years. Cleaning. Taking her mother to doctor's appointments when Millie was working. Let me tell you, Eleanor Hall is a dragon lady."

"We actually met them a few days ago. I can see that Millie's mom could be tough."

"Understatement," Jessica said wryly. "But Millie sure appears to be playing grieving widow today."

To be honest, it took me a moment to locate Millie. Of course, the wide-brimmed hat with black veil did make it harder to see her features. She was dressed in a black crepe, tunic-style jacket and a black skirt that stopped at her knees. The whole ensemble was very Queen Elizabeth and did seem a bit over the top. Especially for the funeral of a mere acquaintance.

She did look like a grieving widow. Was there more going on between Millie and Cliff than the occasional hello at the supermarket.

"Did Millie know Cliff well?"

"Who knows. I can tell you this, Millie has a lot of money. Inherited from her father. He had a shipyard and made a lot of money. That would make the old spinster very attractive to a guy like Cliff."

I studied Millie again. She clutched a white handkerchief in her hand at the ready for any tears, but right now she spoke calmly with a woman I didn't recognize. Then I heard Millie's mother call to her in that distinct raspy and demanding voice. Millie excused herself from her chat with a slight bow and disappeared out of sight with her mother.

"I tell you, this town is so dull, people will try to turn a funeral into the social event of the season." Jessica sighed as if she could hardly bear the predictability and mundaneness of it all.

I smiled with what I hoped was sympathy, but my attention was already back to the mountain of a man with Frances. His grim expression said he was still irritated, his arms crossed over his barrel chest. Frances leaned close to him and talked quietly, but whatever she was saying didn't seem to be soothing his annoyance.

"Would you excuse me for a moment?" I said. "I need to speak to Frances Robichaud about the celebration of life."

"Oh sure," Jessica said readily. "I'd love to have a moment to chat with Oliver."

Oliver gave me a look, silently imploring me not to leave him. I smiled sympathetically, but headed across the lawn. I had no doubt he could handle Jessica. I'd seen him handle swarms of Haley and Jake fans with no problem. One flirtatious Mainer with a desperate desire for a more exciting life should be a piece of cake for him.

Instead of going directly up to Frances, I skirted around a group gathered near them, trying to look as nonchalant and unobtrusive as I could. When I was a few feet away from her and the hulking man, I stopped with my back to them. I took my cell phone out of my purse and pretended to be looking at something as I tried to block out the chattering group in front of me.

"I just don't see why you would do this," the man muttered.

"I just think it's the right thing to do. It's a respect thing," Frances told him, her voice low and calm.

"When did he ever respect you?" the man growled.

There was a moment of silence, then Frances said, "Mac, no matter what happened between Cliff and me, he was still Karen's father."

I paused my pretend texting. This was Mac. I stepped back a little to get closer.

"Karen told me she doesn't even want to do this. She saw what he did to you. What he did to me."

Frances didn't respond again for a second, then when she did, I couldn't make out what she said. I took another step back, the heel of my strappy sandal sinking into a hole. Arms flailing and cell phone flying, I struggled to regain my balance, then I just braced myself for a hard crash onto my butt. But before I could make contact with the ground, a strong arm came out of nowhere and tugged me upright and against a hard body.

"I'm starting to think you need one of those plastic bubbles to keep you safe," Dean said wryly, his face just above mine. I could smell mint as if he'd just finished eating a candy. Or maybe in his physical perfection, that was just the natural scent of his breath.

I blinked up at him, breathless. "I think you might be right. But I'd probably fall down inside that too."

Instead of being sympathetic, he nodded in agreement. "Or roll down a hill."

He made sure I was steady, then he released me to go retrieve my phone.

While he did that, I glanced around to see that Mac and Frances were watching me. I smiled awkwardly, then moved away from them. Aside from thinking I was a klutz, they didn't seem to notice anything unusual, but I decided any chance for more info was probably lost now, so I walked over to Dean.

He held out my phone. "Did you get any good dirt?"

I frowned, glancing down at my phone, not sure what he was referring to.

"You need to work on your eavesdropping skills if you are going to make a go of this detective thing."

"I wasn't eavesdropping." Crap, was I that obvious?

Dean raised an eyebrow, but didn't say anything more, so I took the moment to play my boss card.

"Is the pub ready for the celebration of life?"

He didn't rise to my bait. "Yes, I left Dave and Janelle there to get things ready. So, it's all under control."

I nodded, realizing I should have known that. Dean always seemed to be in control. "Great. Thank you."

He nodded.

"And thank you for saving my butt." I meant it literally, but I realized he would probably take that as a reference to the fact that he was still pretty much in charge of the pub.

He nodded again, and I wasn't sure how he took it.

"Okay," I said, suddenly feeling completely inept. A bad eavesdropper. An inexperienced pub owner. "I'll see you later."

"Later."

I scanned the groups of people, who had thinned out as more people had entered the church. Oliver stood at the bottom of the steps, waiting for me.

"You managed to get away from Jessica," I said softly as I reached him.

"Yeah, as soon as I said I wasted most of the money from my hit show on drugs and gay strip clubs, she suddenly found someone else who she just had to speak to."

"See, I knew you could handle her."

"Oh yeah, that trick always works with gold diggers." He held out his arm and we started up the stairs to the church.

The inside was packed, so we stood at the back against the wall. A kaleidoscope of light reflected on the white and oak pews from the stained glass windows that lined both of the other walls. The casket and dozens of large floral arrangements sat at the front of the spacious area, along with a robed minister who nodded and spoke to people as they passed him to view the open casket. The sound of organ music played softly.

"Do you have to do that?" Oliver whispered, staring at the line of people waiting to say their final respects to Cliff.

"We should. Isn't that what you are supposed to do?"

He grimaced more. "I've never seen a real dead person."

"What about your friend Moe's funeral?" Oliver had a musician friend who died in a freak stage-diving accident.

"He was cremated. I saw his urn. It had a picture of him etched on it. Although the image looked more like Flea than him."

"Mmm," I said sadly. I'd be disappointed if my image looked more like a member of the Red Hot Chili Peppers than myself.

I'd never seen a dead body either, suddenly thankful that was

MURDER DRAMA WITH YOUR LLAMA   105

the case. But that was about to change. I grabbed Oliver's arm and tugged him to the line.

A low hum of quiet conversation filled the church. I tried to make out what people were saying, but with the organist playing, I could only make out a word here and there, Still, it was better to focus on that than thinking about seeing a dead Cliff.

All too soon, given how many people were there, we reached the white coffin. Cliff lay inside in a gray suit and a rather jaunty red tie. He looked surprisingly good for a dead man. There was artfully applied color in his cheeks. His thin hair was brushed neatly. He even seemed to have a crooked little smile on his lips.

"He still looks like a player," Oliver whispered.

I elbowed him lightly.

"What, I think he'd appreciate that."

I couldn't argue. We looked at him for a moment, neither of us exactly sure how long was long enough.

"Can we go?" Oliver finally said.

I nodded. I started to step away from the casket, when I caught a flash of something under Cliff's neatly folded hands. I leaned closer.

"What are you doing?" Oliver mumbled, desperate to get away from the body.

"Do you see that?" I whispered, gesturing with my head.

Oliver looked around like he just wanted to flee the church, but then he sighed and moved closer.

"It's a ring," Oliver said.

I nodded. Someone had tucked a gold wedding band under his crossed hands, just the edge of it visible. The way it was shoved in there, it looked like someone must have placed the ring there today. Had Frances done that? Had she kept his wedding band all these years? Or maybe someone had been planning to marry him, then he died.

Who might have been planning to marry Cliff?

EIGHT

WHEN WE STEPPED into the pub, I realized I should have given Janelle and Dave better instructions. It looked like a middle school dance. There were balloons in clusters at the entrance and over by the bar, and there was a table set up with a punch bowl. An actual punch bowl. I had been convinced those only existed in prop warehouses and yet here was one, running free in the wild.

"Wow," Oliver said. "I feel like a fourteen-year-old Hilary Duff might appear at any second."

I winced. "Should we ditch the balloons before anyone gets here?"

"Well, isn't this lovely?" a woman's voice asked.

I turned and saw it was Frances. Her face didn't display any anger. She looked genuinely pleased with what she was seeing.

"Is this what you had in mind?"

She nodded. "Yes, absolutely. It's a celebration of life. Celebrations have balloons. It reminds me of when Cliff and I went to prom together."

"Oh, for cripe's sake," Karen said as she entered the pub. "What is all this nonsense?"

"I'll have the servers start bringing out the food," I said and gestured to Oliver to follow me. I didn't need to hear more bickering between the mother and daughter.

"I hope they have lobster rolls out," Oliver said.

Mourners, or celebrators, I wasn't sure which at this point (for reasons having nothing to do with my decor), started to trickle in. I was heading to the kitchen to check on the food situation when Brandy came out from the back with a charcuterie tray. Obviously the staff already had everything under control. I felt a little superfluous. Then again, why would they need me? They'd been running the restaurant before my arrival and I knew nothing about food service.

That made me feel momentarily defeated, but then I saw Hannah with an older woman. I went over to her and said hello. She looked awkward in black jeans and a black T-shirt, as if she'd been told she had to wear black and that was all she had. She looked like she should be on a stage crew instead of in a pub filled with older people.

"I'm Sophie," I said to the woman Hannah was with.

I'd lost Oliver at the cheese tray.

The woman stuck her hand out. "I'm June Martin, Sunny's best friend." Her voice was gruff but her eyes filled with tears. "I really miss that old gal. It's a pleasure to meet you. I would have come around sooner but Cliff chose now to go legs up."

That was certainly one way to put it. "It's so nice to meet you too. It seems like my grandmother had a really great circle of friends here."

"She was a special lady. The only one not taken in by this old fool's nonsense."

"Which old fool?" I asked, not following her.

She waved her arms around. "Cliff."

It occurred to me that in spite of being in her sixties, June was a strong woman. She was nearly six feet tall, and had thick muscular arms that had seen their fair share of physical labor. It wasn't difficult to imagine her having the strength to bash Cliff over the head, though I had no idea if her calling him an "old fool" was affection or actual disdain.

"My grandmother didn't have a crush on Cliff?" That made me like her even more.

Hannah snorted. "That's so gross."

June glared at her. "My granddaughter Hannah was never fond of Cliff."

"Oh, Hannah is your granddaughter? She's helping me out with Jack, which is so helpful to me. I'm new to llama ownership." I turned to Hannah. "Cliff wasn't your favorite?"

"No. I was glad when he dumped Grandma." She crossed her arms over her chest defensively, like she knew she was about to get yelled at but didn't care. "He was a user."

June didn't correct her. "Sophie doesn't want to hear about my romantic stupidity." But then she turned to me and kept speaking. "It's true. Cliff was great at profiting from his relationships. We all thought he was a dog but somehow it would be different with us. Sunny never fell for his crap. They had a brother-and-sister type relationship and he was a great help with her llamas."

That would all explain how Hannah had come to be friends with Jack Kerouac.

"I'm sorry things didn't work out with you and Cliff." Was that a reason for her to kill him?

"My bank account is safer this way, trust me. I thought I was immune to his charms but I fell for the old con just like half a dozen before me." June nudged Hannah. "Come on, we need to make the rounds so we can get out of here. I'm only here so I don't look like a horrible person."

"I'll see you tomorrow, Sophie," Hannah said to me with a wave.

"For sure, thanks. Nice to meet you, June."

She just nodded, but then she looked me up and down. "You do have the look of her. Though black isn't your color. Washes you out."

With that insult, she walked away. I frowned and walked over to Oliver. "There are a lot of angry women in this place for a town called Friendship Harbor."

"Devious ones, too. I just saw some woman pouring vodka into the punch. I called her out on it but she just laughed and said it was all in fun." Oliver held up his plate. "They do have lobster rolls. You should taste this."

I was too distracted to think about a lobster roll. "What did she look like?"

"I don't know. Honestly I was very busy checking out the food. Have you ever had a whoopie pie?"

I ignored him. Oliver was food obsessed.

"Did you tell Dean we need more punch?"

Oliver looked at me blankly. "No. Was I supposed to?"

"That was supposed to be for the non-drinkers. If someone wants alcohol, they can order from the bar." I turned to the beverage table, a bit panicked. "You didn't leave the spiked punch out, did you?" There were several women and men standing around ladling the beverage into their cups.

"Whoops. That did not occur to me, I have to admit. I did taste it to confirm though. Definitely vodka."

Wonderful. "Seriously?" I shook my head and made my way over to the punch. "Excuse me, um, can I just get in here and take that? It needs to be refilled." It was only halfway empty but I needed to say something. I muscled my way into the group and picked up the bowl.

"Best damn punch I've ever had," Mac said, tossing a whole cupful back.

Yikes.

"I agree," Millie said. "It's very refreshing. This is my third cup."

Double yikes. Time to fess up.

"I would take it easy on the punch if I were you," I told her. "It's come to my attention that someone thought it would be entertaining to spice it up with vodka."

Mac gave a loud snort of a laugh. "If that don't beat the Dutch. No wonder I like it so much."

"Oh, dear," Millie said, even as she took another sip. She was still wearing her veil and she lifted it slightly to fully get the cup to her mouth. "I'm not much of a drinker."

"Who was the rascal who spiked it?" Mac asked. "I want to shake his hand."

His casual attitude surprised me. It really was like a middle school dance. What was next? We were going to have a photo back-drop fall and we'd see someone making out?

I sincerely hoped not.

I didn't want to accuse anyone without proof, so I just said, "It was a woman, but I am not sure who."

I probably shouldn't have even given that much information. Instantly, Mac started speculating. "It had to be June. That's her MO."

The no-nonsense woman I had just met did not seem like a mischief maker.

"Is it odd that I can't feel my lips?" Millie asked.

I didn't respond to either of them. I just tried to carefully walk into the kitchen with the punch sloshing in the bowl. It was like trying to carry a fish tank. Some of the red liquid splashed up onto my cleavage.

In the kitchen I elbowed past Dave and dumped the whole thing into the sink. He eyed me like I was nuts, but fortunately Dave was not a big talker. He didn't say a word.

Brandy was a different story. "What are you doing?" she asked. "Did someone sneeze in that or something?"

"My friend Oliver saw someone pouring vodka into it. He tested it and confirmed. Unfortunately, Millie and Mac both drank it and who knows who else."

Her mouth fell open. "Someone put alcohol in it? Who would do that? This is a funeral!"

Reassuring to know she thought it was odd and not some small-town standard. "I think we should just walk around and offer a tray of water glasses to guests so we don't have a repeat of this."

"Good idea." She nodded approvingly. "I'll get Janelle on it. How many people are out there?"

"About thirty at quick guess." I needed to get back out and mingle and eavesdrop, though maybe with more skill than I had earlier.

The first person I spotted when I came back out was the sheriff. I gave him a smile. "Hi, Sheriff."

"Hi, Sophie. And please, call me Justin. I'm off duty." The smile he gave me in return was warm enough to make me take notice.

Huh. Interesting.

He was in a dark slim-fitting suit that was clearly new and following the modern trend of not having a man drown in a boxy jacket and pleated pants. Like his uniform, it revealed a man who was in shape. No doughnuts for this sheriff.

"Did you know Cliff personally?" I asked, seeing an opportunity to press for more information.

But Justin Pelletier was staring at my cleavage. "Sheriff?" I asked, dryly.

His head snapped up and he had the decency to look sheepish. "You've, uh, got something there." He pointed at my chest. "It looks...sticky."

Startled, I glanced down. There was a red trickle of punch down my chest. "Oh!" I looked around for a napkin. "It's punch."

He was holding a plate of appetizers and he had a napkin underneath, which he pulled out. "Here you go."

"Thanks." I mopped my cleavage and tried to remember what the heck I had been about to say. While I fished around for polite conversation I glanced around the room, still swiping at my chest. I felt responsible for the success of this event, not wanting to be the woman who arrived from California and failed. But by all indications everyone was having a good time. There was actually a lot of laughter.

Then my gaze landed on Jessica and June. They were not laughing. In fact, they both appeared to be talking quite heatedly. June gestured to something at Jessica's side, although I couldn't make out what. June grabbed up a punch cup from the bar and strolled away as if she'd made her point and was done. Jessica watched her go, then walked away as well. Great, with all this spiked punch flowing, there was bound to be a barroom brawl by the end of the night.

Then I spotted Oliver. He was bent over the table with the display of photos of Cliff and was writing on something. He handed it to a woman in her twenties with a flourish. Was he signing autographs?

"To answer your question, yes, I knew Cliff personally. He was buddies with my grandfather. He also owned a lot of property around town and frequently had disputes with his next-door neighbor. A couple of times I got called out there to find him brandishing a shotgun in his neighbor's face. Cliff was what people around here call a character."

"Where did Cliff live? Close to here? It seems he was around my grandmother's house a lot."

"That's because he liked to drink." A dry voice spoke behind me.

I turned and saw Dean. "Is that so?"

"Yep," he said, hands in his pockets. He was wearing black jeans and a button-up shirt. "Sheriff." He gave Justin a nod.

"Dean."

Okay. No love lost there, clearly. They looked like they were about to challenge each other to pistols at sundown.

"Cliff lived on Maple," Justin said, picking up the thread of our conversation.

"So right by where he was found, then?" I almost said "murdered" but stopped myself in the nick of time.

"A few blocks away, yes."

"And was his neighbor around? The one he hated?"

"Excuse me?" Justin's eyebrows went up. "Why?"

Dean looked amused. "Subtle," he murmured under his breath.

"What are you talking about?" Justin asked Dean.

"Sophie thinks Cliff might have been the victim of foul play, versus death by llama."

I glared at him. I wasn't sure why it had to be a secret from the sheriff but it certainly felt like Dean had prematurely tipped my hand. "I never said that." Well, not exactly. I had thought it. I'd just never said it to anyone but Oliver.

It seemed super rude to suggest the sheriff didn't know what he was doing in his career so I was going to deny it.

"You know, since Sophie is an amateur detective," Dean said. "Or played one on TV."

"Well, Karen Robichaud requested an autopsy be done, so I'll guess we'll have the answer to that sooner than later. The report should be in today actually."

I blinked. "Karen requested an autopsy? But I thought she was completely convinced I let a killer llama on the loose."

Justin shrugged. "I guess she wants to make sure she's directing her anger at the right culprit whether it's an animal or a human."

That basically eliminated Karen as a suspect, didn't it? She would want to discourage medical probing and closer police examination. She would ride the llama story hard. Which she had been the day Cliff had died. Had something changed her mind? Or someone?

Without warning there was a high-pitched shrill cry. "No, Mother, I won't calm down and I'm not a stupid woman!"

We all turned to see who the voice belonged to.

It was a very clearly intoxicated Millie leaning heavily on a high-top table and waving her plump arm around.

Her mother was perched precariously on a stool at the table, looking like she might topple off at any given second. She spoke to her daughter, but we couldn't hear what she was saying.

Just then a disembodied voice came over a loudspeaker, announcing to the whole room, "Welcome to Wednesday night trivia."

I shot a furious glare toward Dean. "Really? You didn't reschedule trivia night?"

Dean shrugged helplessly. "I told you the people in this town take their trivia very seriously."

A man near us turned on his barstool. "I'm here for the trivia."

I blinked. How had this memorial gone so far off the rails?

"Alright, are all our teams ready to go?" the disembodied voice said. "Here is your first question... What famous Italian was reputed to have slept with over one hundred and thirty women?"

"Cliff wasn't Italian, was he?" I overheard a woman say to her friend as they passed us clearly looking for the now missing punch bowl.

"This is literally the best funeral I've ever been to," Oliver said, appearing by my side. He had yet another plate of lobster rolls. "It's like a reality show."

He sounded way more gleeful than was appropriate for the occasion. I shot him a look, which he ignored.

"What would you know about love?" Millie continued. "You've never loved anything or anyone in your entire life, including me!"

People were gawking and murmuring behind their hands. The whole situation was getting awkward.

Justin shoved his plate at Dean. "Take this, will you? I should go talk to Millie."

Dean took the plate and frowned at it.

I opened my mouth to chastise Dean for basically making fun of me in front of the sheriff. I still hadn't decided if his teasing was good-natured or mean-spirited. The jury was still out on Dean.

"And the answer is Casanova. It looks like all the teams got that one right. And on to the next question. What is a flock of crows called?"

I gaped around feeling like things were going downhill at a very rapid pace. I was pretty sure this was going to be the pub's one and only celebration of life event.

Justin had positioned himself between Millie and her mother, but it didn't appear the portly woman liquored up on vodka and fruit punch was calming down. I shifted closer to them so I could hear the conversation.

"You have no idea how much I have tolerated because of that woman," Millie said, poking Justin in the chest to punctuate her words.

"Oh for God's sake, Millie, try to get some control over yourself," June said, picking up a glass from the table and polishing the whole contents off in one swallow. Great, another old lady getting sloshed on the liquored up punch. "It wasn't like Cliff didn't dupe half the women here into thinking he loved them."

Millie turned her drunken outrage toward June. "You don't know anything about me and Cliff."

So, Millie had known Cliff much better than she had initially said. I tried to catch Oliver's eye, but he was too busy eating another lobster roll like it was popcorn and he was watching a particularly exciting movie. Just beyond him, I noticed Jessica Grace watching the scene with the same entertained expression.

"Oh, believe me, Millie, I know a lot about old Cliff and just about all of his women," June said. And with that, she grabbed her granddaughter's arm and left the pub.

The room was silent.

"Okay, it looks like most of the teams got this one right," the disembodied voice said. "A flock of crows is called a murder."

Millie burst into tears, and Frances moved forward to put an arm around her. "Why don't you let Mac take you and your mother home."

Millie nodded, looking as if all her drunken anger had left her totally deflated. Mac obediently moved to help Eleanor Hall to her feet. For once, the ancient woman didn't say a word, which I already got the impression was rare for her.

"I can take the ladies home," Justin said.

"I've got it. I think I've had enough *celebrating* for the night myself," Mac said, his tone filled with sarcasm.

Justin nodded, although he still looked like he thought he should handle seeing the old women home. Frances continued to hug Millie as the foursome walked slowly toward the pub door.

But before they could exit, Hannah came running in, screaming. "Help! Someone please help me! My grammy just passed out."

NINE

PASSED out would have been the best-case scenario, but as I watched the ambulance race away, lights flashing, I didn't get the feeling that was the situation. I'd overheard the EMTs using terms like massive myocardial infarction. Unresponsive. Flat line. All phrases for not good.

"Well, tonight didn't end nearly as amusing as it started out," Oliver said, clearly shaken.

I looked around. All the attendees, even the die-hard trivia players were standing on the sidewalk outside the pub. Everyone looked stressed. I spotted Hannah. I was most worried for her. The poor kid just witnessed her grandmother suffer a massive heart attack. Thankfully, she was standing with a man and a woman that I assumed were her parents. The woman hugged her close to her side, while the man held the woman's hand. They were all pale and seemed in shock.

Justin talked with two of the police officers that arrived on the scene with the ambulance. He nodded at something one of them said, then headed over to speak to Hannah's family.

"What should we do?" Oliver said, looking around at the crowd that now broke off into small clusters, talking among themselves.

"I guess we just go back in," I said, although I didn't know if that was the right answer. It seemed unlikely that people would want to continue Cliff's memorial with all the drama and this horrible turn of events. But I still wanted to help my workers clean up, and frankly I was too rattled to remain still. Helping them seemed like the best way to distract myself.

When we walked back into the pub, Brandy and Janelle were already cleaning off the tables. They looked up as we entered.

"It didn't look like that went too well out there," Brandy said, a tray of plates and glasses balanced on one hand.

I shook my head. "No. It sounded like a very serious heart attack. I'm not sure June survived."

Brandy nodded as if that was the answer she expected, then headed to the kitchen.

I moved to help Janelle load another tray. Even Oliver started gathering up the clutter. To my surprise, some of the patrons filed back in, taking seats at the bar. Although I couldn't really blame them. I felt like I needed a drink after what just happened.

But I focused on clearing the tables, even as my mind whirled. June was dead. Just like that. And I now knew for certain Millie had been involved with Cliff. Or at least infatuated with him. Did she kill him? Given how upset she was, it didn't seem likely. I had to admit, I felt like tonight had created more questions than answers.

I tossed some dirty napkins onto a tray, when I had the sensation of someone standing behind me. I turned to see Justin.

"How are you doing?" he asked, his kind eyes dark with concern.

I felt a little silly having him be so worried about me. After all, I just met June. "I'm okay. How is Hannah?" She was the one I was most worried about.

"She's pretty upset."

"It had to be terrifying."

He nodded.

I hesitated, then asked the question I already knew. "June didn't make it, did she?"

He shook his head, not needing to say anything more.

I closed my eyes, suddenly overwhelmed by the last week. It had been one hell of a week, that's for sure.

Justin cupped a large hand around my elbow. "Let's sit down for a moment. You look like you could use a break. And maybe a drink."

Again, I felt uncomfortable. I barely knew Cliff. And frankly what I'd seen had been borderline creepy. I just met June. But I did feel pretty wrecked.

"Yeah," I agreed, giving him an appreciative smile. "I think I could use a glass of wine and a little calm."

Oliver watched us as we headed to two empty barstools, but he continued to help Brandy and Janelle. I guess I'd have to pay him for his help with more lobster rolls and a side of fried clams. Then again, Oliver had his surprising moments of kindness.

"You must be wondering where on earth you moved," Justin said with a lopsided smile as he took a seat next to me.

"It has been pretty bananas," I admitted.

"It's been pretty wild for us too," he said with a shake of his head. "Would you believe last month the craziest thing that happened was a streaker at the women's softball game?"

"A streaker?" I laughed. "I thought that went out of style in the seventies."

"We are a little behind the times here."

I laughed, then asked, "It wasn't Cliff, was it?"

He chuckled. "Surprisingly, no."

"That was rude of me, wasn't it. I guess I shouldn't say something like that at his celebration of life."

Justin cast a look around. "I think that's pretty well over."

I nodded, seeing that most everyone had left. Brandy came out from the back of the kitchen and joined us. "What a night. What can I get you?"

"I'll have a pinot noir."

"An Island Dog Ale would be great."

"I'll have what he's having," Oliver said, taking a seat on the other side of me.

"So," I said. "It really does seem like Cliff managed to con a lot of women in this town." Even though I was freaked out about everything that happened tonight, I couldn't stop myself from wanting to find out more about Cliff.

Brandy set drinks in front of us. "I heard he conned several women out of a lot of money. Personally, I always liked him. Sure, he could be a bit of a lech, but I found him pretty harmless. And he always tipped well."

"And I don't really know," Justin said. "Like Brandy, he always seemed like a nice enough guy to me. But that doesn't mean he wasn't a dog. I will say that I have heard plenty of rumors."

"Like?"

Justin shrugged as if he wasn't really comfortable talking out of turn. He really was a nice guy. I liked that. A lot.

"Well, I heard that he cheated on Frances with a wealthy widow who owns a huge mansion in Bar Harbor," Brandy said, clearly not having the same hang-up about sharing juicy gossip. "I heard this woman was like in her late seventies. And this would have been back when he was in his forties."

Janelle joined in, leaning on the bar beside Brandy. "And there were also some rumors he dated a woman who used to summer up here from Massachusetts. He conned her out of thousands and thousands of dollars."

"And clearly he was involved with Millie," Brandy added, her expression saying she never saw that one coming. "She inherited a ton of money from her father. Although she was clearly keeping that on the down low."

"Probably because she's so under her mother's thumb," Janelle said. "Old Eleanor probably would have locked her in the house if she had known."

Dean came over and joined the conversation. "When I was a kid Cliff dated my aunt."

"Wow, Cliff was one busy man. I hope he put some of that money into Viagra stock," Oliver said. "Soph, the old guy had more action in a week than you have in a year."

I choked on my pinot noir. "Oliver!" I could feel my cheeks heating up. "That's not really funny."

I mean, he wasn't wrong. But it wasn't funny. Especially not in front of both Dean and Justin. I wasn't thrilled about Brandy and Janelle hearing my love life was pitiful, either.

"It's not true," I added. "I date," I said defensively. "I absolutely date."

"It was a joke," Oliver said. "Chill."

Except that there was enough truth to it that I'd overreacted and now everyone knew it was true.

"Good," Justin said. "Then I can invite you to dinner and hope you'll say yes." He gave me a smile.

Oliver made a sound of approval. "Slick, Sheriff. I like your style." He turned to me. "Say yes to the nice man, Sophie. He has good teeth."

"He does have good teeth," Janelle said.

Now I was officially embarrassed. But I was intrigued by the sheriff. I wouldn't object to getting to know him better. "Is that an actual invitation?" I asked him. "Or a theoretical?"

"It's an actual invitation. Are you free Saturday?"

I nodded. "Yes. I'd love to go to dinner with you."

"Fantastic. We can go to Bar Harbor."

"Oooh," Brandy said. "Fancy. I love it."

Dean abruptly moved away from the bar and went into the kitchen without a word to anyone. I couldn't figure that guy out for love or money.

"Well, I should be heading out," I said. "I need to check on my llama."

"I need to get a llama so I can use that line," Janelle said. The server was in her twenties, with a cute pixie haircut. "I could get out of literally everything I don't want to do. No one can argue with needing to tend to a farm animal."

Dean reappeared in the doorway to the kitchen. "You can't get out of cleanup. Can you stop gossiping and clear the food?"

She made a face.

That was definitely our cue to leave Steamy's.

I stood up. Oliver did the same.

We said our goodbyes and got out of there, heading through the back room to the yard.

Oliver started to say something but I made a shushing gesture. I had a feeling that the walls of the Victorian were thin and the people in the pub could possibly hear what we were saying.

When we got outside, I used an exaggerated whisper that had him rolling his eyes. "Don't you think it's strange that so many people would show up to Cliff's funeral and celebration of life when they didn't even like him?"

"No. People do that all the time. Face it, Soph, you're searching for a murder when maybe there isn't one. Just a small town with a whole lot of gossip." He didn't even bother to whisper.

"I know this was murder. Jack couldn't do it. You agreed yourself the timing was off."

"But what if Cliff just took a fall?"

I shrugged, noncommittal. I didn't want to argue with Oliver about it. "Poor Hannah. No one should witness something like that at her age."

"I'm not sure I needed to witness any of that at *my* age. And L.A. has the rep for drama queens." He shook his head.

I opened the gate to the yard by the shed and let Jack out of his pen. He came bounding into the yard and straight up to Oliver, who indulged him by rubbing his head.

"He's going to miss you," I said, amused. "I'm going to miss you too." Oliver was due to leave on Monday.

"Nah." He waved his hand in dismissal. "You'll be busy with Sheriff Sexy and Surly McSteamy. But I'll definitely miss you. We should have chairs out here, by the way. And wine. I feel like Jack could use some hangout time."

"That sounds fun. You get the chairs and a couple of those jar candles that my grandmother has all over the house. I'll go get some wine from the pub."

"Excellent plan." Oliver saluted me and left the yard.

I went into the shed and got some hay out for Jack and put it in the pen for him. He started munching merrily away while I went for the wine. Going in the back door, I heard low voices in the kitchen, but assumed it was Dave and Janelle.

There were still at least a dozen people in the pub, which impressed me. Trivia night was no joke. Brandy waved to me and I asked her for a bottle of pinot noir to go. She bit her lip like she wasn't sure she was allowed to do that, but then she said, "Well, you are the owner of this place, so what am I worried about?" She gave me a grin.

"Thanks. You can ring it up and I'll pay for it if that's easier." I didn't want to complicate the inventory.

She looked relieved. "Okay, thanks. That's probably best for right now." But then she added, "The nasty business with June broke up the party a bit and there are tons of leftovers in the kitchen. Why don't you make up a couple of plates for you and Oliver? We're just going to pitch it."

"Thanks, Brandy. Oliver has a crush on the lobster rolls."

"I noticed. I also noticed that he eats constantly and weighs about eighty pounds." She shook her head in disgust. "I can't look at carbs without gaining five pounds."

"Same. Damn men and their metabolisms." I went into the kitchen but then stopped short when I realized it wasn't Dave and Janelle in the back at all. It was Frances and Mac.

What on earth?

I crouched down so they wouldn't see me and listened to their conversation. Frances sounded highly agitated.

"You heard what the sheriff told Karen! Cliff could not have been killed by that stupid llama."

Hey, now. I was offended on Jack's behalf.

"The autopsy showed it was blunt force trauma, all right, but with something much smaller and more forceful. A llama only has two toes and soft pads, you know that. He said it was more consistent with something like a hammer."

"Calm down," Mac said in a soothing voice. "What's done is done."

"It's very upsetting to have the sheriff poking around in Cliff's business and Karen is on some insane quest for justice. What are we going to do?"

"Absolutely nothing. There is nothing to do but ride it out. It will all blow over."

That sounded one hundred percent to me like Frances and Mac were very concerned about getting busted for Cliff's murder. I wanted to wait it out and see what else was said but my thighs were screaming and without warning I lost my balance and knocked into a steel rack holding mixing bowls.

The rattle was very loud and by the time I scrambled to my feet to explain that I'd dropped an earring, Frances and Mac were gone, obviously bolting out the back door. It was right at that moment that Dean opened the kitchen door and smacked me in the backside with it.

"Sorry," he said. "Brandy told me you wanted a bottle of wine. I told her to charge you at cost."

"Thanks," I said, a little breathless. I tried to discreetly rub my screaming thigh muscles. "She said to take some leftovers."

He nodded. "Good night, Sophie."

"Good night."

I gathered the food and the wine and hotfooted it back to the yard. Oliver had managed to haul out two kitchen chairs and a delicate round Victorian side table that I thought had been in the bathroom. It had a candle on it burning brightly in the growing darkness. "I need to string up fairy lights," I mused. "Between the shed and the guesthouse."

"That would be divine." He took the wine from me. "Should we bother to change out of our funeral finest or shall we be pretentious?"

"I don't need to change." I sat down and watched Jack, who

was loping along the fence perimeter, sniffing here, and sniffing there. "Because I've ruled Karen out as the killer and have two new suspects."

"Can I at least pour the wine before you dive into another round of theories?"

That was wise. I held out my glass, and fortunately Brandy had opened the bottle for us when she rang me up. Oliver tugged out the cork with a satisfying little pop, then filled my wine glass, which he'd also snagged from my grandmother's house, stopping at nearly the brim of the large goblet.

"Whoa, I want to be able to get the intel out to you," I said, eyeing the huge amount of vino. "You know I start getting giggly after two glasses."

"If this whacked-out night doesn't call for a giant glass of wine, then I don't know what would."

He had a good point. I took a sip and waited for him to fill his own. He took a long sip, then shifted in his chair, settling in for my story. "Okay, hit me."

I explained what I'd overheard.

"Wow, that does all sound really shady. Do you think Frances and Mac killed him together?"

I shrugged. "They both have a lot of reasons to want Cliff dead."

"But why now."

"That is a good question. Maybe something was about to happen that would mess up their plans. Like Cliff was going to get married. What if Frances was still in Cliff's will? She said they were still actually married. If he finally went through with the divorce and married someone else, that would make his new wife the beneficiary."

"Mmm," Oliver said, giving me an impressed look. "That definitely makes sense."

We both sipped our wine. Jack lifted his head from eating grass, twitching his ears as if he heard something.

I found myself looking around at the darkness just beyond our candlelit circle. I shivered. The air was cool, but I didn't think that was it. What if someone was listening to us just like I'd been listening to others? The idea was creepy.

"You know maybe we should finish our wine inside," Oliver said suddenly, clearly thinking the same thing I was.

"I agree." I rose gathering our glasses and the wine. Oliver moved to get Jack, who thankfully followed him back to his stall with little prompting. Almost as if he wanted to be inside too.

I looked around again as I waited for Oliver to return. Another chill crept over me, even though I could hear a few voices and music coming from inside the bar. I knew I was probably overreacting, and it wasn't like I was alone, but I watched the shed, willing Oliver to hurry up.

Fortunately, he returned quickly.

"Let's get the table and chairs in the morning," Oliver suggested as he picked up the plate of leftovers. Trust Oliver not to abandon food.

"Good idea." We hurried back to the house, an unexpected blast of sound from Jack sending me jumping in the air.

"Geez," I breathed. The second we got inside I slammed the door and locked it behind us. "I think I'm getting paranoid."

"I think we're from Los Angeles. We're smart. Or at least, I am. You can be a little gullible."

I made a face at him. It's not like I could argue with him. "I resemble that."

TEN

"WAKE UP, LAZY BUTT."

I groaned, shoving my tangled hair out of my face as I rolled over. Oliver stood in my bedroom doorway, already dressed and looking far too cheerful. How was this fair? We'd finished our bottle of wine in the kitchen and Oliver had opened a second bottle we'd found in the back of the fridge. I had three glasses to his six and yet I felt like I'd been the one kicked by a llama.

Not that my llama kicked anyone. That was a fact now. Still, I felt awful.

"Why are you up so early?" I grumbled, closing my eyes again.

"It's almost noon."

I blinked. Really?

"But I've been up for hours. I let Jack out to graze. I took a walk down to the water. And I found this."

He strode to the edge of my bed and waved a piece of paper in my face. I frowned at it, trying to focus my bleary eyes on what it said. Finally, I snatched it out of his hands, squinting to read the flowery lettering.

"There is a blueberry festival. Today. Food, rides, crafts, and fun."

I handed the paper back to him, wondering why he bothered to show me the flyer.

"That does sound fun."

"So, let's go. We need some fun. And I want to get the whole Maine feel."

I closed my eyes for a moment, then nodded. I immediately wished I hadn't. My head pounded and a wave of nausea hit me. Why oh why was I such a freaking lightweight?

"Food, rides, crafts and fun, Soph. I love blueberries."

"Who doesn't?" I grumbled back.

Oliver's excitement wasn't diminished by my grumpy reply. "I'll give you a minute. I'll make some coffee and some toast."

I started to nod again, but caught myself. "That would be great actually."

"Excellent," he headed out of the room, calling out as he headed downstairs. "Food, rides, crafts, and fun. It has two of my favorite F words."

Despite my misery, I managed a smile. He did have a point. I loved all those things too. Well, maybe not the ride part. I swallowed back another wave of nausea.

"Okay, Soph," I said aloud. "You can pull yourself together."

I sat up and groaned. "And avoid pinot noir for the foreseeable future."

FORTUNATELY AFTER A LONG, hot shower, I managed to feel somewhat human, although I was less than peppy as I walked into the kitchen. As promised, Oliver had coffee and toast waiting for me.

I collapsed on one of the stools and forced myself to take a bite of the dry toast. It was like paste in my mouth, but I forced it down. Then another bite and another. By the time I finished one slice, my roiling stomach had calmed.

"You are a lifesaver," I said after a sip of my sweet, creamy coffee.

"Well, how many times have you been there for me."

"So many," I said dramatically, then smiled. I finished my coffee, then took a deep breath. "Okay, I'm ready. Let's find out what a blueberry festival is like."

We stepped out of the house to discover it was a bright, beautiful day. The sky was blue, birds sang. I breathed in deeply. This really was a gorgeous place.

"Hey, guys."

I spotted Hannah over by Jack's enclosure. She wore high-waisted, denim shorts and a baby blue T-shirt that said, Be Kind. On her feet were her pink Converses.

"Hi, Hannah," I called to her, heading in her direction. "I like your shirt. I have one like it."

She smiled, but I could see the sadness in her eyes. Of course, she was sad. The poor kid just lost her grandmother.

"Are you here to hang out with Jack?"

She nodded. "Then I'm meeting some friends at the blueberry festival."

"Hey," Oliver said with a wide grin, "that's where we are heading too. Is it as amazing as it sounds."

Hannah didn't look quite as excited as my friend. "Yeah, it's pretty cool. My grandmother used to sell her blueberry jam there."

My heart ached for her. I couldn't help myself, I had to give her a hug and to my surprise she hugged me back.

"Do you want to walk there with us?"

She nodded. "Yeah, that would be cool."

"Great, let's see what this festival is all about. Did you already check on Jack?" I asked, realizing Jack probably should be let out. It was a beautiful day and the llama needed to graze and get some exercise.

"Actually, Miss Sunny used to bring Jack to the festival," Hannah said.

"Really?" I tried to imagine walking the large animal around the festivities.

Hannah nodded. "She'd let kids pet him and last year he was crowned Blueberry King."

I shot Oliver a surprised look. "Blueberry King. So Jack is a local celebrity?"

"Kind of," Hannah said as if I should already know this.

"I say we do it," Oliver said. "I think I saw some sort of muzzle thing hanging in the shed. Hannah, do you know how to put that on him?"

Hannah laughed. The sound made me laugh too. It was good to see her not so somber.

"It's not called a muzzle. It's a harness. And I have seen Miss Sunny put it on a few times. It looks pretty easy."

Oliver looked impressed. "Okay, then let's do this."

We headed into the barn. After a bit of trial and error, we got the nylon, rainbow-colored harness onto Jack. I had to give the animal props, he waited patiently as Oliver and Hannah fiddled with it. He must really like the blueberry festival too.

"How many newbie owners does it take to harness a llama?" I joked, although we all looked at our work proudly. Jack made his purring noise.

Hannah located his leash and we started on our way.

"I hope Jack wins king again," Oliver said, holding Jack's leash.

Jack loped beside him, already looking very regal, if I do say so myself. Many other people were walking up Main Street toward the fairgrounds, where the festival was held. Several people greeted us and the llama. I was glad to see the locals who'd heard of the false accusations against Jack didn't seem to fear him.

"So how did he win Blueberry King last year?" I asked Hannah as we stopped to let two elementary-age kids and their mother pet him.

"He was up against Dean Jordan and Sheriff Pelletier," Hannah said as if that should be answer enough. "Oh, and a chicken named Stu."

I laughed, imagining the two men's reaction to losing against a llama. The chicken probably didn't care.

"Clearly the best man won," Oliver said as we started walking again.

The fairground was more like a large field with dirt pathways zig-zagging around tables and booths. A small Ferris wheel had been set up in the middle along with an ornate gold and mirrored carousel with flashing lights and antique horses spinning in a circle. Beyond that, there was a bouncy house filled with jumping, squealing kids. A band was set up in a covered bandstand playing classic rock favorites.

"I feel like I'm walking onto the set of a Hallmark movie or something," Oliver said, his delight obvious. I had no idea my friend could be so sentimental.

"Hey, mister, can I pet your llama?" said a little blonde boy with something blue and sticky smeared around his mouth.

Some of Oliver's glee faded at seeing the messy state of the kid. "Okay, but don't get him all sticky. He's here to win Blueberry King."

I rolled my eyes and moved over to crouch beside the little boy. "Of course you can pet him. His name is Jack."

The boy grinned. "Jack," he said as if trying the name out or committing it to memory. He reached out a grubby hand and patted the animal. Despite myself, I did wince when he left a blue, gooey smear on Jack's white fur.

He tapped the llama's side a couple more times, then dashed off to join his calling mother.

"If he ruined Jack's chances to bring home the crown..." Oliver said with a disgusted shake of his head.

Hannah giggled.

"I have wet wipes," I told Oliver, because I didn't want him to fixate. Which he would. I pulled the pack out of the small purse I had put over my shoulder and across my body. "Here."

Oliver diligently cleaned up Jack and then like a kid, handed me the dirty wipe. I rolled my eyes yet accepted it. Making a face, I shoved it in my purse.

We wandered through the event, stopping here and there to

look at crafts. I bought a rock painted like an owl that I thought would look good on the kitchen windowsill. Oliver bought a green baseball hat that had the term "Maine-iac" embroidered on it. It sat perched sideways on his head as he and Hannah shared a container of chocolate-covered blueberries. I also bought some home-made blueberry jam from a sweet woman in her thirties, who seemed to have a dozen children scampering around her table.

"Okay," Oliver said to Hannah. "You are the old pro here. What should we make sure we don't miss here?"

"You don't want to miss the doughboys," Hannah assured him. "And the pie-eating contest."

Oliver's eyes widened. "They actually have a pie-eating contest?"

Hannah nodded, laughing at his excited expression.

"I've died and gone to Castle Rock."

Hannah gave him a puzzled look, clearly not getting his Stephen King/Stand By Me reference.

"Okay, we have to see what time this amazing pie-eating contest is going to happen," he said.

"I think I saw a chalkboard with a list of events back by the entrance," I said. "You guys go check that out. I'm going to keep looking at the crafts," I said. The two scampered away with Jack in tow, Oliver looking more like the excited youth than Hannah.

I laughed and turned my attention to a booth filled with quilts and pot holders and other hand-sewn items. I touched the edge of one of the beautiful quilts, a kaleidoscope of star shapes and bright colors. I recalled my mother's horror at the idea of me buying a quilt and felt amused and defiant. She'd hate this.

"That's one of my favorites."

I turned to see Millie sitting in a lawn chair in the shade of her booth. She wore sunglasses even though there was no sun on her and I immediately felt her pain. I just only started to not have a dull aching in my own head. Booze was the devil, at least for us wimps.

"I didn't see you there," I said with a smile. "Did you make all these?"

She nodded, dropping the book she'd been reading to her lap. I noticed it was a romance novel and I felt a wave of sadness for the older woman. She was clearly a romantic, and she'd thought she'd found her grand romance with Cliff. Only to have him die, while also discovering he was a dog who had made plenty of other women feel the same way for him.

"Yes," she said. "It's something to keep me busy."

Again, I felt sorry for her. Millie didn't have a life she deserved. That was obvious.

"They are just beautiful. How much is this one?" I gestured to the quilt I'd been admiring moments earlier.

"That one is three hundred dollars."

I tried not to react with sticker shock. Three hundred dollars. That seemed like a lot, but then again, this quilt was made by hand. That was hours of work. And tons of detail.

"I'd like to buy it." Okay, I didn't exactly know how I was getting paid from the pub. Or even how much. Another topic Dean always managed to avoid with me. But I did have some savings and I had made some decent tips from waiting tables. So why not. The quilt would look amazing in my grandmother's house.

I was just finishing paying Millie, who seemed pleased that I'd made a purchase, which made me happy, when Oliver and Jack reappeared.

"I lost Hannah to her friends," he said, looking like the kid who'd been ditched at the playground. He stroked Jack's snout. "Oh hello, Millie."

Millie managed a small smile. "How is Jack enjoying the festival?"

Before Oliver could answer, a grumpy, raspy voice we all knew and dreaded, I glanced at Millie, some of us more than others, grumbled, "Get that stinking beast out of my way."

We turned to see Eleanor being pushed in a wheelchair by Jessica. Jessica rolled her eyes and maneuvered the old lady into the covered stall, near where Millie sat.

"No worries, Eleanor, the llama isn't in my way," Jessica said, sounding far more solicitous and sweet than her expression revealed.

"Miss Eleanor," I said. "Are you feeling okay?"

"Don't call me Miss Eleanor," she snapped. "This isn't the damned old South here."

"I'm sorry," I said immediately, and then wondered why. I wasn't the rude one here.

"And I'm fine. My daughter insists that I use this to embarrass me." She thumped the arm of the wheelchair angrily. "I'm perfectly capable of getting around on my own."

"Mom," Millie said, her tone soft and meek. "You know I feel better when you use the chair on uneven ground or when you will be walking for a long time. It makes me feel better."

The old lady humphed, but didn't argue.

"Well, I think we should probably go find those doughboys," Oliver said to me, not hiding that he wanted to get away from the tension in the little stand.

"Right," I agreed readily. Even Jack pranced a bit in place as if he wanted out of there too.

"Thank you for this beautiful quilt," I said to Millie, holding up the white trash bag she'd given me to transport the quilt home in. "You do such amazing work."

"Thank you," Millie said sincerely and again, I felt sorry for the older woman. I suddenly had a huge appreciation for my mother. She could be a little judgy and she definitely had her pretentious moments, but she ultimately always supported me and I never doubted her love for me. I got the feeling poor Millie rarely got a kind word from her crotchety mother.

"Did you find anything interesting on your walk?" I heard Millie ask her mom as we strolled away.

"The same crap they have every year," Eleanor said grumpily. "Did you bring my knitting? I need something to do if we are going to be stuck here all day."

"No, Mom, I didn't."

"I can go get it for you," I heard Jessica offer in her overly friendly voice. "I have my key. I'll be back."

"Jessica is trying to get out of there too," Oliver whispered as we headed to the food truck advertising corn dogs, hand-cut fries, and the much coveted doughboys.

Once we got our doughboys, which was a thick circle of fried bread dough served hot and covered in powdered sugar, we found a spot in the shade and sat in the grass.

"I've found nirvana," Oliver moaned as he tore off a piece of the pastry and popped it in his mouth.

I had to admit it was seriously delicious, crispy and chewy at the same time with just the right amount of sweetness. "Hannah wasn't lying."

We munched on our new favorite treat, watching the other festival-goers. Behind us, Jack nibbled on a patch of clover.

"I'm going to miss this place and you," Oliver said.

I leaned my head on my friend's shoulder. "I'm going to miss you too."

We sat like that for a moment, then Oliver hopped up. "Okay, let's go, I have a pie-eating contest to win."

He held his hand out to help me up. "You're really doing it?"

He nodded, spinning his baseball hat backwards in preparation. "I've been preparing for this day all my life."

I shook my head, chuckling. I couldn't deny that. Oliver had mastered the art of overeating.

"Come on, Jack," I said, snagging his leash. "We have to cheer Oliver to victory."

THE SUN WAS GETTING low in the sky by the time we started home. Oliver proudly wore his first place ribbon on his berry-stained T-shirt, having finished his pie in one minute and fifteen seconds. I wore Jack's crown for Blueberry King, very proud that he'd defended his title, although Dean and Justin hadn't been there to run against him again. I also had my bags of crafty treasures and the beginnings of a sunburn. Overall, a very successful day.

"I think I have to lie down," Oliver groaned as he walked with me to return Jack to his shed. "I'm stuffed."

I didn't doubt that. He ate his weight in fair foods. "Go on in. I'll finish taking care of Jack."

He looked very thankful. "Are you sure? I feel like I've reached a new low in my life."

"I got this." I led Jack into his stall, then worked on the buckles of his harness. He nibbled at his crown as I worked, knocking it off my head.

"See you in a bit, then." Oliver staggered out of the barn, probably tipsy on sugar and carbs. I finished caring for Jack, then hung his crown on a nail on the shed wall. "Good job today, big guy."

The llama rumbled in response, making me laugh.

I was still smiling when I locked the gate to his pen. Today had been wonderful. No thoughts about Cliff. No wondering if there was a murderer in our midst.

"Sophie."

I turned to find Hannah walking across my backyard.

"Hey, Hannah, did you have fun on the rides?" She and her friends had joined me to cheer on Oliver during the pie-eating contest, but they had taken off again after his epic win to explore and get on the rides.

She nodded. "My friend Billy rode the carousel fifteen times in a row, then barfed in a trash can near the bandstand."

I nodded with approval. It sounds like Billy was committed to his work.

"So, I was wondering if I could ask you a favor," Hannah asked, suddenly seeming a little timid.

"Of course."

"Would you mind coming with me to my grandmother's house? I'm supposed to go there to feed her cat. My mom is allergic, so we have to leave him at Grammy's house until my aunt can take him when she comes up from Portland for the funeral." She paused as if ashamed to admit that next part. "And I don't like to go in there alone. You know since what happened."

I totally got that.

"Yes," I said immediately. "Of course, I'll go with you."

I didn't want Hannah being any more freaked out than she already must be. Plus, I might get the opportunity to peek around at June's house. Maybe there was something there that would reveal more about Cliff's death. She did say she knew about all the women Cliff had been involved with. And just like that, my day off from super-sleuthing was done.

JUNE'S HOUSE WAS A CUTE, little Cape Cod with two dormers and shingle siding. Hannah shoved a hand into the front pocket of her shorts and pulled out a key. She unlocked the front door and stepped into the dim, silent house.

As I followed, I couldn't blame her for not wanting to do this alone. There was something eerie about the stillness of the house. It got a little less creepy when she flipped on the hallway light, but I still felt a little weirded out. I could only imagine how Hannah felt.

"I'm going to go look for Winston. I think he's scared being here alone."

"Do you want me to come too?"

She shook her head. "He's usually just hiding under my grammy's bed. I can get him to come out. He might not if a stranger is there."

That made sense. But I still gave the girl props for heading up the shadowy stairs by herself. I'd had to do it so many times on Murder, She Texted I'd gotten wary of it, especially since the crew had started to find it hilarious and would jump out of random props.

As soon as Hannah disappeared, I headed to the room to the left of the door. It was a small living room with a wood-burning stove and plaid furniture. Very New England. But aside from some magazines and books stacked neatly on the table, there didn't seem to be much in the room that would be particularly personal. So I continued through that room to what was supposed to be a dining room, but June had set this area up as a small office with bookshelves, an antique oak desk, and a computer.

Score.

I flipped on the light and carefully began to look around the room. I scanned the shelves for any books that might look like a diary or photo albums. Anything personal. I did find a photo album, but after a quick flip through it, it seemed to be only pictures of her child and grandchildren. Nothing unusual. I eased it back onto the shelf.

Then I moved to the computer, jiggling the mouse. To my surprise the screen lit up. Still on. I cheered in my head. But of course it was asking for a password. What would an older woman make as her password? I quietly typed in Hannah. No luck. I deleted it, and pursed my lips, trying to think of any other options. Personally, I tried to keep my own passwords simple, because otherwise, I forgot them.

Her cat.

Carefully, I typed in her cat's name. Winston.

To my shock, it worked. And even more to my shock, her computer screen unlocked to reveal an open email. I scanned it. Oh my God, it was an email. From none other than Cliff Robichaud.

I quickly scanned the typed message. It was essentially a Dear Jane letter. Cliff had broken up with her over email. And he'd said millennials were addicted to their computers and social media. A breakup via email seemed pretty harsh, even by millennial standards.

Overall, the email was pretty nice, as far as digital breakups went. He was sorry to end things with her. He enjoyed their time together. But he'd met someone else. Okay, that had to be hard to read. And he'd fallen in love and they were planning to marry. Okay, yeah, this was a rough letter.

But he was planning to marry. And that definitely meant the ring in his casket had been a wedding band.

"Found him," I heard Hannah call. I heard her footsteps moving through the upstairs. Fumbling, I felt around the side of the computer screen and found the on/off button. I pressed it and the screen went dark. I then hurried as quickly and quietly as I could to snap off the light. I walked back into the living room, poking my head out to look up the stairs. Hannah appeared with a huge orange and white tabby spilling over her arms.

The cat didn't look particularly stressed, although I'm sure he was wondering where his owner had disappeared to.

"Aww, look at that big, handsome boy," I said.

"He's a big baby. I wish we could keep him," Hannah said, nuzzling her cheek against his giant feline head.

"Can one of your grandma's friends take Winston?"

"Probably."

Hannah didn't appear to find anything odd about the fact I'd been in her grandmother's office room, which was good. A little guilt tightened my chest, but I pushed it aside. After all, I wasn't snooping just to be a snoop. I was trying to figure out what was going on in this town.

"CLIFF WAS PLANNING TO GET MARRIED," I announced as I walked into the living room to find Oliver collapsed on the sofa.

"What? Where have you been? I was getting worried."

Not so worried that he'd tried to look for me, but he did look miserable. So I guess I could forgive him.

"I went with Hannah to feed June's cat. And while I was there, I did some investigating. I found an email from Cliff on her computer. He broke up with her via email. Pretty cold, right?"

He didn't answer that. Instead, he struggled to push himself upright, moaning as he did. "Wait, you looked at her computer?"

I nodded, grinning proudly. "I even guessed her password."

"Sophie, this is getting a little too much. You can't go through someone's private stuff. Even if she's dead."

My grin faded. "Someone killed Cliff. We need to try and find out who it was."

He gave me a look like I was hopeless. Then he grimaced and rubbed his unusually distended belly. "But don't you think the police are back on this? I'm sure Justin knows about the autopsy. I really think you should leave this up to them."

"But I'm plucky, determined, and able to see a mystery where others saw none."

He gave me a worried look. "Are you describing your character from your TV show?"

"That's how they described me in the series descriptor on streaming services."

"That's how they described your character. Not you personally. Soph, I'm starting to worry about you."

I waved my hand as if that would brush off his concern. "So you don't think there is an actual mystery here?"

"I do," he said grudgingly. "But I think we should stay out of it."

I frowned at him, disappointed in his lack of can-do attitude.

He fell back onto the pillows of the sofa with another groan. "Okay, so what do you think we should do next?"

"Well, I haven't quite gotten that far. But I will."

Oliver closed his eyes. "I'm sure you will, but not tonight. Pie-eating victory comes at a heavy price."

I gave his prone body a sympathetic look. Okay, I would take a break for the night. Besides, I did need to figure out what the next move was anyway.

Would it be weird if I went and binge watched Murder, She Texted? I decided it would and settled onto the bed in the guest room and watched Criminal Minds instead.

Shemar Moore could definitely teach me a thing or two.

Even if I learned nothing, having him in bed with me was not a bad thing.

ELEVEN

"WHAT IF JUNE WAS MURDERED TOO?" I said upon entering the kitchen the next morning to find Oliver at the kitchen counter, eating a heaping bowl of cereal. "By the way, I'm glad your stomach feels better."

"Last night was rough, but all good now. Well, you know, until you decided one murdered local wasn't enough."

I looked up from pouring my coffee and gave him a stern look. "Any murder is too much."

He shook his head. "True. But how did we get to the possibility June might have been another victim? You heard the EMTs say it was a massive heart attack."

"I know, but something about the timing seems very strange to me." I'd stayed awake until the wee hours of the night going over and over the suspects I had. And that's when I'd started to think about June's untimely demise. "She seemed just fine when I talked to her earlier that evening."

"Well, that's how heart attacks happen sometimes. We've all heard of people just dropping dead from them."

I nodded, joining him at the counter. I reached for the cereal. "But did you hear what she'd said to Millie as she was leaving? She said she knew a lot about all the women Cliff had affairs with. What if that made someone nervous?"

Oliver took another bite of his cereal, chewing slowly as he considered my theory. "So what could someone give a person to cause a quick and deadly heart attack?"

"I have no idea. But thank God for Google. I'm also going to see if Justin has any info on June's death while we're on our date."

"I was hoping you'd just, you know, have fun on your date," he said wryly. "But I'm starting to think this detective stuff is fun for you."

It was. But I didn't say that, afraid it would sound pretty morose.

"I'm just going to see what I can find out." I took a big gulp of my coffee. "But first I have to get ready and head to the pub for the lunch shift. Brandy asked me to fill in for her."

"And maybe Dean will actually have time to teach you how to, say, run your own pub."

I made a face at him as I headed out of the kitchen. Not likely.

"HOW DO I LOOK?" I asked Oliver as I stood in front of the mirror in the bedroom, ready for my date with Justin. I had gone into my grandmother's closet and pulled out a seventies sundress in a blue floral pattern.

"Fantastic," he said. "I'm loving this vintage vibe you have going on. You should do this more often."

"Thanks. I like it too. It feels like the Maine version of me. A little more relaxed."

"Being away from the constant rejection of Hollywood will do that for you." Oliver sat on the bed and gave me a stern look in the mirror. "Now young lady, be home by midnight and no inappropriate touching."

I laughed. "You sound totally creepy right now in the role of my father. I don't like it."

"I don't think I like it either. So stay out all night and have a banging good time."

"I'll settle for somewhere in between." I was looking forward to the date. "Despite you humiliating me about my lack of social life."

"It was a joke, I'm sorry."

"Too soon, Oliver. Too soon. It's only funny if it's not true but it is true." I hadn't intended to stop dating. But after my boyfriend, Alex, and I split on reasonably good terms when he decided to join a cruise ship entertainment cast, I'd been in a funk.

Lost relationship, lost job. Not a banner year for me.

But despite a murderous hiccup I still felt positive that Maine was going to be a fresh start for me.

Justin drove a truck, which didn't surprise me, but was still an adventure to climb into in a dress. He also opened the door for me, which was very gentlemanly and unexpected. That clued me in that maybe I had been dating the wrong men if an opened door startled me.

"Are you planning to stay here in Friendship Harbor?" Justin asked me, clearly curious as he drove us to Bar Harbor. "That's a big change from L.A."

"I was on the fence about it, honestly. I committed to being here for several weeks with the intention of it being permanent. But knowing I could bail if I really needed to." I smoothed down the front of my grandmother's sundress. "I'm going to stay though. One hundred percent. I needed a reset button on my life."

Justin glanced over at me and gave me a smile. "California's loss is our gain."

That made me laugh. "That may be overstating things. I'm an out-of-work actress with zero skills in the restaurant business. As of today, I'm more liability than asset. What about you? Did you grow up here?"

"I sure did. I left and went to UMaine for four years, then came home and went to work at the sheriff's department. I never felt the need to live anywhere else. If I want to travel, I go on vacation."

"It's good to know where you belong. I'm working on that. I grew up in California and I love the weather, and I did love being an actress but I don't know if it's what I was meant to do forever." I made a face. "Clearly not, since I've been out of work for six months."

"I watched a couple episodes of your show. Why do I get the feeling you've taken on that role here in Friendship Harbor?"

The sheriff was definitely on to me. "What role?"

"Amateur sleuth."

I couldn't exactly deny it. "Well, I know a murder when I see one. I knew there was no way my llama could have killed Cliff and to be totally honest, I'm not so sure June died of natural causes either."

Justin pulled into the parking lot of a clapboard waterfront restaurant.

"Oh, this is beautiful," I said. There were sailboats in the marina to the right of the building and the water was calm and endless.

"June didn't die of natural causes," Justin said.

I whipped my head around. "What? How do you know that?"

"I can't give you a lot of details because this is an open investigation. But I can tell you she died of a high dose of nifedipine."

"And what is that?" My heart was racing at the thought that there truly was a killer on the loose in this town.

"It's a blood pressure medication. But when given in huge amounts it can cause sudden and deadly heart attacks. But according to her doctor, June didn't have high blood pressure and was never prescribed the medication."

"So someone killed her?"

Justin shook his head. "We don't know that. It could have been an accidental overdose. She might have taken medication meant for someone else, gotten confused. We can't draw any conclusions until everything has been thoroughly investigated."

"Whose medication would she have taken?" I asked. That made no sense.

"She's the one who cleared out your grandmother's personal possessions. There are people who hoard medication and who self-medicate rather than go to the doctor. This isn't a town where people are eager to step into a physician's office. They think all those tests are scams meant to make money. So maybe June felt like she had high blood pressure and she nicked Sunny's pills and was taking them incorrectly."

"I suppose that is possible." I had no clue if my grandmother had been taking high blood pressure pills but none of what Justin said was out of the realm of possibility. Yet I knew in my gut there was more to this than the obvious accidental overdose.

I needed to search the internet and find out how many pills she would have had to take in order to have a heart attack.

Justin opened his car door but he turned back, expression serious. "I promise you, though, we'll look into this. You don't need to, Sophie."

He was clearly a mind reader or I had a lousy poker face. "Uh-huh. I just think it's an odd coincidence right after Cliff's murder. But it seems Cliff had a lot of enemies."

"Cliff had a lot of money. Sometimes that's the most obvious motive. He turned a lot of heads when he built that brand-new house a few years back."

Interesting. "What's going to happen to it? It goes to Karen?"

Justin nodded. "It was up for sale actually as of last week, right before he died. I'm not sure how all of that will shake out. I would imagine Karen will still sell it."

"Huh." I was mulling over what all of this meant.

Sighing, Justin stepped out of the car. I opened my door before he could come around and open mine. I felt guilty having him be so attentive when I had exactly zero intention of staying out of June's death or Cliff's murder.

Instead, I just changed the subject and chatted about the weather, asked questions about the marina, and spent a lot of time marveling over the menu. I was nervous and it was obvious. After ordering, I excused myself and went to the restroom to wash my hands and calm my jitters. I took a few deep breaths, watching myself in the mirror.

This was a role I could play. Woman on a dinner date.

On my way back to my table I saw Mac dining in a cozy back corner, away from the stunning view. He was with a woman. There was no way to walk past him without being totally obvious, since there was nothing but the kitchen in the part of the restaurant they were seated, but I knew that head of hair. It was Frances Robichaud, with her tightly permed hair the color of a bottle of merlot. There was no mistaking anyone else for her.

To my surprise she leaned forward, and though I couldn't see her expression, she tenderly stroked Mac's cheek.

Couple alert.

"Your chowder arrived," Justin said as soon as I returned to the table.

"Oh great." I sat down and tried to focus on my food and Justin. Not easy when I wanted to keep sneaking glances at Mac and Frances.

"Are you okay?" Justin asked, regarding me over his own spoon of clam chowder.

"Yes," I said quickly. Too quickly.

So with determination and a big smile, I focused all my attention on Justin. My mystery solving could wait long enough for a great meal and friendly chat.

"THANK YOU FOR A GREAT EVENING," Justin said, pulling his truck in front of the pub.

"No, thank you. I think that baked stuffed lobster was life altering."

He laughed. "It was pretty good. But the company was better."

I appreciated his compliment, but I wasn't one hundred percent feeling interested in him and I wasn't sure if it was the move, the murder, or something else entirely.

"It was nice to spend some time with a local," I said. "I need friends here in Friendship Harbor." Which I was pretty sure that's all I wanted us to be, at least for now. Hopefully he would get the subtle hint.

Justin smiled, and I couldn't miss his gaze dropping to my lips.

Okay, nope. I definitely was not ready for a kiss even though he was a great guy, smart and funny and definitely handsome in that rugged Mainer sort of way. I didn't want to drop an "it's not you, it's me" on him, even though it was, so I gave him a big smile and reached for the door handle.

"Thanks again! We should grab coffee sometime, my treat." I meant that. I could really see myself being friends with Justin.

His eyes lifted to mine, reading my face. I had a cheerful expression on it, or at least I hoped I did. That was the look I was going for and I was an actress, after all. I clearly succeeded, because I couldn't miss the flash of disappointment in his eyes.

Justin returned the smile and nodded. "That would be great, Sophie."

I opened the door and slid down from the seat, tugging at the skirt of my dress as I did. "Good night," I said.

He nodded again, and I shut the door.

I stood on the sidewalk, watching as he pulled away. After his taillights turned the corner, I debated if I should have just given him the straight truth. I wasn't ready to get romantic, but I did want his friendship. This was all about creating a life I could love, not finding a man to love.

Feeling confident it was the right move for me, I headed up the lawn to go check on Jack. I'm sure the llama was sound asleep and probably didn't even want my attention, but checking on him always made me feel good. I loved caring for my new and unique pet.

I flipped on the light as I entered the shed.

"Hey, sleepy Mister Jack," I called as I walked up to his stall. As expected, the big guy was nestled in amongst his straw on his folded legs, eyes closed. He reminded me of some zen, meditating guru.

I smiled and turned to leave, when I spotted something against the far wall of the shed. An object covered with a gray canvas tarp. Hmm, I'd never noticed that before. I walked over and tugged at the heavy cloth. It slid to the ground and revealed a bicycle. It was mint green with a basket and a bell. Then I realized behind that was another one, this bike powder blue with a light perched on the top of the front fender. They both looked like something from an old movie, vintage and cool.

Good to see I had wheels, even if it wasn't a car. I really was going to need to return to L.A. and drive my car back to Friendship Harbor. The car was currently parked in my parents' driveway, which I'm sure was not thrilling my mother. She would interpret that as clutter.

Having a bike would allow me to explore easier, and would give me some exercise.

Closing up the shed, I went into the apartment.

Oliver was lying on his back on the sofa with a book held up over his head, reading. "Why are you home so early?" he asked. "Did the date suck?"

"No. But it was just dinner. I didn't want to give him any false impressions."

"Or let him see you're hot for your pub manager?"

I couldn't argue with that, though I had zero intention of acting on it. "There is that. But listen, I have to update you on the current situation."

Patting his legs so he would move them, I sat down next to him and prepared to update him on all things June and the tangled web of Friendship Harbor romances.

TWELVE

"WHILE THIS HOUSE isn't large, it does have some really amazing amenities," the real estate agent said as she opened the front door to Cliff's house.

Okay, so I definitely wasn't following Justin's advice and staying out of Cliff's murder. However, how dangerous could it possibly be to look at his house when it was on the market? It was noon and I wasn't trespassing. Nothing I was doing could technically be considered interfering with a murder investigation.

"I don't need a lot of square footage."

"Are you two planning to have children?" she asked.

Oliver made a choking sound. I had to give the agent props. She smelled blood in the water. A "couple" from California might mean a quick sale for her. Unlike me, she had an amazing poker face. There was no doubt she had to have an opinion about us, but her face didn't reveal a thing.

Patricia was in her fifties, polished, pleasant.

"No," Oliver said firmly.

That was certainly true.

"Then this will be a great fit for you. Three bedrooms, two and a half baths, one floor for easy living. Just look at these gorgeous bamboo floors." She led us into Cliff's house.

"Do you think Cliff was dating her too?" Oliver murmured under his breath. "Definitely his type."

"Shh." I waved my hand wildly at him.

Patricia's phone rang, the ringtone a hair metal band from the eighties.

"Oh, sorry about that." She silenced it, then pointed to the fireplace. "Gas, which is a rarity here. Everyone loves their woodburners, but I think you can agree flipping a switch is much better than chopping wood."

Oliver opened his mouth and I could have guaranteed he was going to make a joke about wood, so I cut him off before he could speak.

"I totally agree, Patricia."

Her phone rang again.

"Will you excuse me for a minute? I'm so sorry. Feel free to look around."

"Of course," I said, secretly delighted.

I instantly went down the hallway, searching out a home office. That's where I had found information at June's and where most people kept their paperwork. When Oliver tried to follow me, I whispered, "Keep a lookout for Patricia for me."

"Am I supposed to cough or fake sneeze when she's coming?"

"Just call me."

He rolled his eyes but he went back into the living room.

Cliff's house was not what I was expecting at all. It wasn't a lodge look, or a seventies style, both of which somehow came to mind when I envisioned Cliff's tastes. It was very traditional. Fussy, almost, but attractive. Either Cliff had a love for antiques or a woman in his life had decorated the house for him.

Knowing I had very little time to search, I tucked my head into a bedroom. It had nothing but a treadmill in it. I guess Cliff needed to stay in shape to chase women. There might be something of interest in the closet, but I didn't really have time for that. I needed the paper pile.

I found what I was looking for in the second bedroom. It had a desk, a TV mounted on the wall, and a lot of sports memorabilia. The desk was piled high with stacks and stacks of papers and magazines. Shifting through it quickly, keeping an eye on the door, I marveled that Cliff seemed to have kept every piece of snail mail sent to him in the last six months. Who needed this many pizza fliers?

But then I spotted something interesting when I lifted his closed laptop. Sitting on the keyboard was a marriage license. Dated two weeks earlier.

Cliff had been planning to marry Millie.

Well, my, my, my. Who would have thought?

I took a picture with my phone, slammed the lid of the laptop back down and turned to take a peek in the closet. Right as I was sliding the door open I sensed movement behind me. I started to turn, caught a glimpse of a person around my size, then had no time to react before I was hit so hard I fell to my knees.

As I clung to the doorframe, stunned, Oliver came rushing into the room.

"What the hell happened?" he said, sounding frantic. "I heard you moan. Are you okay?"

Gingerly, I touched the back of my head. Patricia the real estate agent was behind him. "I'm okay. But I think maybe we need to cut this showing short."

"Do you want me to call an ambulance?" Patricia asked. "You don't look well."

I didn't want to admit to her that there was an intruder because I didn't want to freak her out or have her think I was nuts. I also didn't want to explain to the sheriff why I was pretending to be a buyer for Cliff's house the day after he had told me it was for sale.

"Can I at least offer you a ride home?" Patricia said. "I know you rode over here on bikes and I'm not sure it's a good idea for you to be on a bike going home."

"That would be wonderful, Patricia, thank you."

Oliver helped me to my feet and despite feeling woozy I put on a brave face. Fortunately, it was an easy ride home. Oliver followed on one of the bikes. We could go retrieve the second one later. I was already lying down on the sofa drinking water when he got there.

"Did you pass out?" he asked. "Maybe you should call the doctor."

"I did not pass out. Someone hit me on the back of the head."

Oliver's jaw jumped. "What? How was that even possible?"

"Where were you?" I asked. "Were you in the living room?"

"No, I was being an amazing friend, as usual. I asked Patricia to show me the backyard to give you more time. We were outside."

"That makes total sense. We must have interrupted the killer looking for something at Cliff's."

"You seriously need to go to the doctor and tell the cops. Did you get a look at the person?"

"What is the doctor going to do? I'm not even bleeding." I dismissed the idea. "I got a quick glimpse from the side. I feel like it was a woman, though I'm not sure why." Had I smelled perfume? It was hard to remember, but my gut was saying female.

"I really think you need to report this to Justin. Whoever hit you could have really hurt you," Oliver said, clearly irritated with my cavalier attitude, which quite honestly wasn't as cavalier as I was making it seem. It was darned scary to be attacked. But it also told me I was getting close to finding out something that someone didn't want me to know.

"Honestly, I'm fine. Just a little bump on the head. Nothing major." Not to mention, I really didn't want to go to Justin right after he asked me to leave the investigation to him.

"Yeah, well, Cliff got a little bump on the head too," Oliver said flatly.

"I'm fine," I assured him, even though my head was pounding a little, but nothing a couple ibuprofen and uncovering more clues couldn't fix. "I think we shouldn't lose any time with this. I feel like we are close."

Oliver sighed, realizing I wasn't going to listen. "You really need a better hobby. Okay, so what do you want to do next, Super Sleuth?"

"Time to go talk to Millie."

MILLIE'S HOUSE was just as I imagined it. A quaint Victorian with a front porch and gingerbread trim around the eaves.

"Why, hello," Millie said as she opened her door, the floral wreath tacked to it swinging close to her newly set, white hair. She smiled, but I could see she was surprised to see us there.

"I was hoping I could talk to you for a moment. About Cliff."

Millie looked hesitant, then nodded. She stood back to allow us inside. As soon as I stepped into her foyer, I could see that Millie's touches were in Cliff's home. She had clearly decorated it for him. I wondered how she got out from under her mother's thumb long enough to be over there.

"Your house is beautiful," I said.

"Oh, thank you. I love decorating."

I smiled, feeling more confident it had been her touches I'd seen all around Cliff's house.

"Would you care for some iced tea? I think I have some soda, too."

"I'm fine. Thank you," I said.

"I'm fine as well," Oliver said, politely.

"Well, please come in." She gestured for us to enter a cream-colored, formal living room with a marble fireplace surrounded by an ornately carved and painted mantel. Over that was an oil painting of wild roses in a vase. The muted pinks and rose colors suited the style of the room.

I sat down on the sofa, suddenly glad I didn't accept the offer for a drink. This room looked pristine. I didn't want the stress of potentially messing up the sea of cream. Especially since my head was still throbbing and I had moments of feeling a little dizzy, but I determinedly ignored it. Oliver sat down beside me looking far more relaxed about the perfect decor.

"So what did you want to ask me about Cliff?"

I'd pondered in a subtle and believable way how to reveal that I knew that she was going to marry Cliff, deciding to go with a lie that I hoped would be believable. Even though I wasn't totally sure the timeline would work.

"I found a letter in my grandmother's house," I told her. "It was from Cliff, and he told her he'd fallen in love and he planned to marry. He said he planned to marry you."

I held my breath, hoping my gamble worked and that my grandmother had still been alive during the time when Millie and Cliff decided to get married.

Millie stared at me for a moment. Crap, the gamble failed. Maybe Grammy didn't even know about their relationship at all. Then the old woman's face crumbled and tears slowly rolled down her pale cheeks.

"Your grandmother was such a wonderful friend to us both. She agreed to have a private ceremony for us in her beautiful garden. Then she passed. And now Cliff has passed." She hung her head, and I could feel her despair. I glanced at Oliver helplessly. He shook his head, not sure what to do either.

Millie's shoulders bobbed slightly as she cried silent tears and I had to reach out to her. I leaned forward on the sofa and took her hand.

"I'm so sorry," I said sincerely. I feel like there was no way this woman could have killed Cliff. He'd been her only chance at escape. To my surprise, she squeezed my fingers in thanks, then straightened.

Materializing a tissue out of her cardigan pocket, she dabbed her eyes and nose. Then she pulled in a deep, shuddering breath. "Thank you. It has been such a terrible time. We were going to marry the day he died. I waited at the courthouse for him, and he never showed up."

The meeting he had said he couldn't miss after giving me the house tour. My heart broke for this poor woman. She finally found her Prince Charming and then he never arrived to sweep her off her feet.

"We planned to marry and then spend our honeymoon in Florida. We were going to look for condos there. It was going to be my wedding present to him."

Some of my sorrow changed to disbelief. Oh, Cliff, you were setting up another patsy. Another wealthy woman to fund your old-age lifestyle. Wow, a total dog to the very end. But I managed to suppress my outrage for poor Millie with another sympathetic smile.

"Did you put the wedding band into the casket with him?" I asked gently.

She blinked up at me. "You saw it?"

I nodded.

"Since I didn't get to exchange rings with him like we planned, I at least wanted him to have it with him." She sniffed again, looking down at her own ringless hand. "He told me he had the most beautiful ring purchased for me. A halo setting with a pear-shaped diamond. I've always been partial to a pear."

Oliver coughed and I knew what he was thinking. Millie herself resembled a pear. "That sounds beautiful." And vaguely familiar. I didn't see a lot of pear-shaped engagement rings in California and yet, I felt like I'd seen one recently.

"I wish I had the ring." She quickly looked up as we heard the front door open. She blotted her eyes again and rose.

"Millie," Eleanor called.

The elderly woman tottered toward the living room door. Jessica Grace was behind her, looking less than thrilled to have been in the crotchety woman's company, although the expression quickly changed as she realized we were all in what I suspected was a rarely used room. I suspected most people had that same look after any amount of time in Eleanor Hall's company.

"Miss Eleanor had a great time at her book club," Jessica said with a bright smile. Like at the festival, Jessica was dressed down, wearing a simple T-shirt and jeans. Her hair was in a ponytail and she was jewelry-free. Without her accessories, she actually looked younger, but there was still a hardness to her.

"I hated the book," Eleanor informed us.

Of course, that could just be a side effect of being with this old bat.

"But you enjoyed the cookies," Jessica said cheerfully, and I didn't miss the subtle criticism in her words.

Eleanor glowered at the pretty blonde. She might be ancient, but clearly she didn't miss it either. Then she turned to her daughter. "You said you had work around the house to do today. What are they doing here?"

"We stopped by to look at Millie's beautiful quilts," I said quickly, feeling the need to get poor Millie out of the hot seat. "Oliver leaves for L.A. this Wednesday and he wanted to get one to take back with him."

Millie shot me a surprised and then thankful look.

Eleanor, on the other hand, shot Oliver a critical look, then snorted. "Why am I not surprised?"

Oliver glanced at me out of the corner of his eyes as if to say, "what the heck does that mean?" It's not like gay men from California were known to be heavily into quilting.

"Millie, is there anything else I can do to help you before I leave?" Jessica said, clearly wanting out of there as much as we did.

"No, I'll just have you come over tomorrow to check on Mom, while I'm at my women's group."

"No problem." She waved and I envied her for her easy escape. "I'll see you tomorrow, Miss Eleanor." The door shut behind her before she even got an answer.

"I'm tired. I'm going to take a nap," Eleanor muttered and shuffled out of the room, but not before her cane lurched slightly, nearly causing her to lose her balance. She caught herself on the doorframe, regaining her balance. So much for the four legs at the bottom keeping her more stable. Millie rushed to her.

"Mom, are you okay?"

"I keep telling you I need a new cane," Eleanor said gruffly.

I studied the cane closer, noticing it was seated crookedly on the floor, one of the rubber feet missing.

"I know. I'll definitely get you one at the pharmacy tomorrow." She continued to hold her mother's arm, and tossed a look over her shoulder. "Will you excuse me for a minute? I'm going to get my mother settled in her room."

"Please, go ahead," I said. "Oliver and I have to go anyway. We can let ourselves out."

Millie nodded and helped her mother down the hallway.

Oliver pulled in a deep breath as soon as we stepped back outside into the sunlight. "Oh my sweet baby James, thank God we are out of there. How does that poor woman live with that nasty witch every day?"

"I have no idea," I said as I started down the walkway to where we'd left our bikes. "But I do not believe for a moment Millie killed Cliff. He was her chance to escape. I bet she would have married him even if she suspected he was using her for her money."

Oliver pushed up the kickstand and got onto his bike. "I would too. And frankly, I'm starting to believe cranky, old Eleanor could have killed Cliff."

It did seem more likely than sweet, albeit pathetic, Millie.

"So I guess that rules out Millie," Oliver said as he allowed his bike to coast down the sidewalk.

It did. And although Eleanor was mean enough, she could barely walk down a hallway without breaking her neck with her lopsided cane. I hit my brakes as a realization came to me.

Oliver took a moment to realize I'd stopped. He braked too, his wheels skidding a little on the tarred sidewalk.

"Soph, are you okay?"

I nodded, grinning like a crazy person. "Yes. I know who did it."

"What?"

But I was already pedaling again, speeding my way back to my house.

Funny, my head suddenly felt just fine.

"Cliff liked younger women, right?" I asked Oliver. "Yet I can almost guarantee he liked money more."

THIRTEEN

"SHE'S HERE," I said, as excited as a kid who'd just spotted their favorite Disney princess at Disneyland. Or in this case, I was looking at the Evil Queen.

Oliver spotted her too. "I really hope you are right about this. Otherwise, we are going to look like lunatics."

"Oh, I'm right." I had no doubt in my mind I was right. Last night, I had pieced together exactly who the killer was and why. In fact, I was so confident, I had contacted Justin and told him to be here tonight too. He had been reluctant at best, but he'd agreed to be present.

In my pocket, the key piece of evidence seemed to burn through my jeans. The odd shape bulged slightly, but I ignored it, certain no one would notice.

Dean watched me walk across the pub, his brows pulled together as if he could immediately sense I was up to something. Which I was. I was about to solve a murder. In fact, two murders.

I sat down at the bar, acting as if I was just another one of the Tuesday, Two for One crowd. Oliver took the stool next to me.

"Hey." I was greeted by Jessica, who sat just a barstool away. "Imagine seeing you here."

I smiled. "Hi. Well, you said Tuesdays at the pub were pretty much the height of excitement in this town. And being the owner, I decided I should probably check it out. Plus, it's Oliver's last night here."

Oliver waved. "Yep, returning to L.A. tomorrow morning."

Jessica gathered up her wineglass and purse and slid down to sit beside me. Tonight, she was back to her glamorous incarnation, and clearly on the prowl. She wore a tight red dress that showed off all her curves and her long, blonde hair was loose, spilling over her bare shoulders. Her lips were stained a deep red, but instead of looking sultry, the color made her hard. And a little desperate, honestly.

It hadn't occurred to me when I'd first met Jessica to ponder too deeply why a woman like her was both single and working for a crotchety old woman. Neither seemed to fit her personality. No, she was more the type who'd want a man to take care of her financially.

A man like Cliff.

Dean appeared, placing a pinot noir in front of me. He set a pint of ale in front of Oliver.

"I like a man who knows what I like." Oliver smiled, which garnered no reaction from Dean other than a raised eyebrow.

I raised my glass. "I think we should toast to you surviving Eleanor Hall."

Jessica grimaced, but did raise her own wineglass. "I'm not sure I want to toast to her, but I can definitely use a drink after spending hours with that old witch." She clinked glasses with both of us and took a long swallow of her wine. Her huge ring was back and glittering.

I sipped mine, then set it down. "How long have you worked for them?"

"Oh, a few years. It seems like longer."

"Bless you," I said and she chuckled.

"I figured that it must have been awhile, because I heard Millie say you had a key. And I don't picture either of those ladies to be particularly trusting."

She regarded me for a minute and I thought for a second I might have already overplayed my hand. Crap. Then she shrugged. "I guess."

She drained the remainder of her glass and gestured to Dean to bring her another one. Good, I was hoping the alcohol would loosen her up a bit. From the corner of my eye, I saw Justin enter the bar. He took a seat at the corner. Jessica wasn't facing him and didn't notice. Another plus. Instead she glared at Dean, who seemed to be taking his sweet time pouring her another glass.

"Do you actually have to stay with Eleanor? Probably not, right? I'm sure Millie doesn't go anywhere," Oliver said almost like he was thinking to himself. Nice improvising. He really was a great actor. I hope he found an awesome role when he got back to L.A.

"Oh, I've stayed with the old witch many times. Millie was leaving a lot there for a while. Although I doubt she'll be traveling quite so much now." She said "traveling" with a hint of sarcasm.

Oh, my theory was so correct. I hid my smug smile behind my glass as I sipped my wine.

Then I shook my head. "I can't imagine. Staying there, making meals, handling her meds. All the stuff you have to do with an older person. That's a lot of work."

Jessica nodded. "And she complained about it all."

I shook my head sympathetically. "I feel for you. And Millie. It cannot be easy for her either."

Jessica chuckled dryly. "Don't let Millie fool you. She's as much of a witch as her mother."

"Really?"

Jessica nodded, grabbing up her drink as soon as Dean set it down. She really didn't like him. I got a feeling he was one of her conquests that got away. I'd have to ask Dean about that one day. Then again, maybe not. I'd already asked about Brandy. I didn't need Surly McSteamy thinking I was obsessed with his love life.

"I would have never guessed that," I said, refocusing on my mission.

"Yeah, she seemed pretty sweet to me," Oliver agreed.

"She's sneaky. And vindictive," Jessica said. "I could tell you some stories. Did you know she was seeing Cliff? Stole him from June, really, if you want the truth of it."

I gaped at her, playing my role of naive town newcomer to the hilt. "Really? I thought she might have been from her outburst at Cliff's celebration of life, but you know, I wasn't really sure."

Oliver nudged my knee with his, but I restrained the urge to nudge him back. We couldn't blow it now.

"She was sneaking around with him. That's why I was watching her mother. Cliff was an old fool but he was not dumb, I'll give him that. He went where the money was."

She took another long drink, and even after she was done, I could see the wine hadn't dampened her anger. If my suspicions were right, and she'd made a play for Cliff, I didn't imagine it felt great that Cliff had chosen a portly woman in her sixties over her.

"So you think he was dating Millie for her money?"

"For sure. But you know what? I guess they deserved each other. Don't let Millie fool you. She was good at playing people. Almost as good as Cliff."

Oh, she was getting close. I could see her anger rising with each question. And I knew that's where she would slip up.

"Good how?" I frowned, pretending to be utterly confused by her comment.

She glanced at me, clearly realizing she was saying too much. "Just good at conning people."

I nodded and calmly sipped my wine. I set the glass down again. Then casually I said, "He did a pretty good job of conning you too, didn't he?"

She shifted on her chair and gaped at me. "What?"

"Well, you thought you were going to take the old guy for all his money, right? But he beat you at your own game. It turned out that Cliff always loved money more than having a piece of eye candy like you on his arm. He went for dollar signs instead of sexy times."

Her blue eyes grew larger. I knew I was right. I knew it. Her shocked reaction urged me on.

"You thought you could out-con the old con artist, but in the end, you didn't get what you wanted. And that really irked you, didn't it?"

She stared at me for a moment, then polished off her wine and grabbed her purse. "I have no idea what the hell you are talking about."

She stood and so did I. I dug in my pocket and pulled out the gray, rubber cork thing I'd found back when we'd been looking for evidence on the trail where Cliff was killed. I set it on the bar top in front of her.

She looked at it, clearly puzzled.

"I found this where Cliff was killed. It's the foot to one of the legs of Eleanor's cane. The cane you stole to kill Cliff with."

She stared at it, then shook her head. "I have no idea what you are talking about. I honestly think you are crazy."

Not even remotely crazy. I was exhilarated to see I was obviously right. Jessica looked agitated and guilty.

"You thought if you used Eleanor's cane to kill him, that would frame Millie. Because let's face it, you really hate her. She stole Cliff away from you, after all."

Beside me, Oliver made a hissing noise through his teeth. "That had to have been a tough blow."

"This is insane." Jessica frantically scanned the pub as if looking for someone to support her on this. Instead, her frenzied gaze landed on Justin. Her face grew pale under her perfectly applied makeup. Justin stood up too and started toward us.

"But unfortunately, June knew you'd had an affair with Cliff. She also knew you had stolen from him. And that was when you decided June had to go. So again, you decided to frame poor Millie. You stole some of Eleanor's medication, nifedipine to be exact, and slipped it in her drink."

"Justin," Jessica said to him as he stopped beside me. "Are you hearing all this? She's as crazy as her grandmother."

I frowned. Again with my grandmother.

"We've already talked to Eleanor Hall," Justin said, his voice calm and certain. "She does take nifedipine. And that rubber cover is the same make as the other ones on Eleanor's cane."

Jessica looked around as if she was debating whether to run.

Not likely in those spiked heels, I thought wryly.

She turned back to Justin, batting her eyes, attempting the only defense she had left. "It wasn't me. It had to have been Millie."

Justin was unmoved by her feeble attempt at maiden in distress. "We already confirmed that Millie was at the courthouse at the time of the murder. I really think you should just come with me and we'll talk about this."

He pulled a pair of handcuffs from behind him. "Now you can come with me easily and quietly without a scene. Or I can cuff you. Your choice."

I could see she was debating whether to resist, or maybe to keep defending herself. But after a moment, she gave in. "Fine. I'll go with you so we can clear all these lies up. But I want my lawyer present."

As she stood up I grabbed her hand and tugged off the huge, sparkling diamond on her finger. Pear-shaped in a halo setting.

"Hey," she snarled at me. Gone was the polished woman I first met.

"I believe this belongs to Millie Hall," I said, holding it out to Justin. "I hope she can finally get it."

Justin nodded, then put his hand on Jessica's elbow and led her out of the pub.

I smiled proudly at Oliver, my adrenaline running high. For a split second there, I'd thought Jessica might try to claw my eyes out.

"You were right," Oliver said. "Though I can't believe you made me pick up a filthy press-on nail at the crime scene and it meant nothing."

"Sorry, not sorry," I told him, cheerfully.

Around the bar a few people clapped, and until that moment, I hadn't even realized anyone had been watching us. Down at the end of the bar, Dean caught my eye, and for a fraction of a second I thought he looked impressed. But then he went back to washing pint glasses in the small sink behind the bar.

"You did it, Super Sleuth."

I did.

And not even as Jennifer Flescher, with memorized dialogue.

As Sophie LaFleur.

FOURTEEN

"I DON'T WANT you to go." I hugged Oliver again. It was going to be quiet and much less snarky without him there.

"I'll be back. You know me, I can't go without pestering you for too long." He smiled, but I could see sadness in his gray eyes. We had counted on each other for a long time. Maybe it was good for us to both go it on our own for a while.

I hugged him again. This time he squirmed away, pretending to be sick of my repeated displays of affection.

"Okay," he said with a deep sigh. "I better go. Who knows what things we could encounter on the wild back roads of Maine. And I can't miss my flight."

"You have to be careful of all the bears and lumberjacks," I reminded him.

He smiled and this time hugged me. Then he got in the Uber.

"Stay safe," he said out the open window. "And keep your mystery-solving to a minimum."

"I will," I promised.

"And don't let Dean push you around. Show him who's boss."

I saluted him. "Aye. Aye."

I could see he was shaking his head as he drove away. For a

moment, I stood there, feeling forlorn. This was it. I was now on my own.

I turned and looked up at the huge Victorian. Grammy's house. Then I smiled. No, my house. I headed up the path and around the lawn toward Jack Kerouac's pen. He was outside grazing on his favorites, dandelions and clover.

"Hey, buddy. I think we are doing pretty fantastic here. Though I have to say, with Oliver gone, you're going to need to step up and be my friend and partner in crime. You'd make a good detective."

Jack twitched his banana ears and continued to eat.

He was a handsome llama. "You just need sunglasses."

He spit on me.

"Or not."

That night, I made another big move. I decided to make Grammy's room my own. I moved my stuff out of the lilac and green guest room, putting my clothes in the dresser. My shoes in her closet along with some of her cool, boho dresses. And the quilt I bought from Millie on my bed. Once I was done arranging things the way I wanted, I wandered over to look out at the backyard. It was quiet. The pub was closed. Only the light from Dean's guesthouse illuminated the garden.

Then I saw him. Dean stood in his doorway. Shirt off. Barefoot. His jeans slung low on his narrow hips. He was looking up at my window. I immediately stepped back, hoping he hadn't seen me. Then I caught myself and moved back. We stared at each other for a moment, then I waved. To my surprise, he waved back.

I smiled to myself and closed the heavy velvet drapes over the French doors.

Now, Dean Jordan was one mystery I didn't think I was ever going to solve.

"Nah," I said aloud to myself. "I'll figure him out eventually."

Feeling good, feeling at home, I crawled into bed and fell back against the fluffy pillows. I lay there for a moment, just enjoying my home.

I rolled over to turn off the light, when my grandmother's still open book caught my eye. I picked it up and flipped through it. A folded piece of notepaper fell out onto my chest.

I sat up and opened it.

Dear Sophie,

If you find this, then I'm going to assume you decided to move into my house. Your house.

My heart melted a little seeing her flowery handwriting and realizing she had reached out to me one last time before she passed on.

I hope you love the house and pub as much as I do.

"I do, Grammy."

I also hope Dean is showing you the ropes. He is a hunk, isn't he?

A surprised laugh escaped me. I glanced back to the now curtained French doors, remembering him shirtless moments before. Oh, he definitely was that.

I'm sure you are finding Jack Kerouac to be the special fellow that I found him to be. But he can be a handful at times too. Still, I think you will grow to love him.

I smiled. He was and I did.

Friendship Harbor is a wonderful place. And I've always been so happy here. I know you will be too.

"I am happy."

Most of the people are kind and helpful. And eccentric too. I'm sure you met Cliff by now.

My smile faded a little. Well, presumably Grammy knew how that all went.

But no matter what you may hear about me, please know it's not true.

I reread the sentence again. What wasn't true?

I love you, sweet girl. And be happy here. I know you will.

Love you always, Grammy.

I fell back against the pillows, clutching the note to my chest. No matter what I hear?

Hmm, not only had Grammy left me a beautiful home and quaint pub and a delightfully quirky pet, she'd just left me another mystery.

Thank you for reading Murder Drama With Your Llama!

Book 2 in the Friendship Harbor Mystery series is available now!
LLAMA SEE THAT EVIDENCE

ABOUT THE AUTHORS

USA Today and New York Times Bestselling author Erin McCarthy sold her first book in 2002 and has since written over seventy-five novels in teen fiction, romance, and mysteries. Erin has a special weakness for tattoos, high-heeled boots, Frank Sinatra, and martinis. She lives with her husband and their blended family of kids and rescue pets.

Connect with Erin:
www.erinmccarthymysteries.com

Kathy Love is a USA Today best selling author of over twenty-five books. She has written in several genres, including contemporary and paranormal romance and horror. Kathy loves all things groovy and retro, especially The Beatles, flower power and disco balls. But she also loves ghost stories, Halloween and New Orleans. What can she say, she's eclectic. Kathy grew up in Maine but now lives in Maryland with her family, three rescue mutts and four rescue cats. It's a full house!

ALSO BY THE AUTHORS

LLAMA SEE THAT EVIDENCE

SOLVING LLAMAGEDDON AND THE ALPACALYPSE

Coming soon:

FA LA LA LA LLAMA

Available NOW from Erin McCarthy

Murder By Design mystery series

GONE WITH THE GHOST

SILENCE OF THE GHOST

ONCE UPON A GHOST

HOW THE GHOST STOLE CHRISTMAS (Holiday novella)

IT'S A GHOST'S LIFE

GHOSTS LIKE IT HOT

Made in the USA
Monee, IL
15 February 2022